The intruder's actions carried information; the Observer was clearly unwelcome. The fellow seized a meter-long rod and swung it violently. Bones ducked quickly enough to save an eye, but got a painful jolt on the left jaw, and a second in the cartilaginous ribs of the same side. Neither blow did serious damage—but both hurt, and neither brought any consolation in the form of new knowledge.

Bones' reaction was almost human; the intruder's third swing was stopped short of its target: one whip-like tentacle seized the stick, and the other lashed against the man's bare chest, leaving a red welt. The attacker fell back with a wordless shriek, uttered two or three more syllables at Bones, and snatched up his breathing mask.

Bones watched with interest. The discovery that this life form could use only gaseous oxygen, rather than nitrates, fitted neatly into his people's old hypothesis that livable planets always went through a stage when they had free oxygen, before they acquired their permanent atmospheres . . .

THE NITROGEN FIX

Dedicated to the students of The Saturday Course—those critical-minded third and fourth graders who were so sure that Bones ought to have

HANDS!

THE NITROGEN FIX

Hal Clement

Illustrated by Janet Aulisio

SF
ace books
A Division of Charter Communications Inc.
A GROSSET & DUNLAP COMPANY
51 Madison Avenue
New York, New York 10010

THE NITROGEN FIX

An ACE Book

First Ace printing: September 1980
First Mass Market Edition: October 1981
Published Simultaneously in Canada

2 4 6 8 0 9 7 5 3 1

Manufactured in the United States of America

CONTENTS

THE NITROGEN FIX

JANET AULISIO

JANET AULISIO

I

Delivery, Delayed

The golden brown sky was losing some of its uniformity, with patches of darker scud starting to show to the west. There was still no wind, and the water was merely choppy, but Kahvi and Earrin were getting more and more uneasy about the kilometer which still separated them from the Canton shore. Milton Island was closer behind, but the cove on its south side would offer little protection if the wind really rose. The rafts, even with their present load, could not be sunk—Newell tissue was far too buoyant—but they could lose the cargo which had taken weeks to collect. The shelter between the Canton shore and the Sayre islets was looking more and more inviting.

"You were right, Kahv. We should have worked around the shore; we could have spared another day or so." Some of Earrin's words were spoken aloud, but since his breathing mask muffled the more subtle phoneme distinctions, hand gestures conveyed much of the thought.

His wife answered with a single, silent nod, not taking her eyes from the shore ahead for longer than was needed to read his signals. She got no particular thrill out of having been right; she had, after all, conceded the weight of the man's arguments and had agreed to try the short cut. Risks always had to be taken; it was merely a question of which ones at any particular time. Spending more time out of reach of an air reserve could also have been dangerous.

This time the raft assembly was much larger than usual and correspondingly harder to maneuver. The Hillers had been emphatic about wanting the very largest supply of metal and glass that could be obtained in two months. There had been no way to increase the rate at which the copper came in from the sea, but Bones had found enough glass on the harbor bottom to load not only the floats usually devoted to cargo but a dozen square meters of extra deck space. It was these new, rather hastily fashioned floats which were the main worry.

Even in poling depth the cluster of rafts was awkward. Earrin and Kahvi had sometimes tried masts and sails, but neither knew anything significant about the art and had to depend on following winds. In deep water they usually used sweeps and Bones.

At the moment the human couple were resting, with their sweeps trailing alongside. The Observer, however, was still at work; the tow lines extending from two of the bow floats were taut, and the raft was still moving slowly westward. If bad weather would only hold off for another hour or so, the cargo might be safe after all. If it didn't—well, Bones could retrieve it from the bottom, but that would be unwise in sight of the Hillers. The group which had ordered this cargo seemed to have a very low opinion of the natives—there had been some mention of "Invaders" during the negotiations, though neither Kahvi nor Earrin had pursued that line of discussion.

But there was no point in worrying about things which hadn't happened; the important thing was action which would get them to the Canton shore and the jail as quickly as might be. Earrin was already taking up his long oar again. Kahvi did the same. The new child was not yet large enough to interfere.

At least there was no wind against them yet. The foamy tissue rode very high, and the whole structure was much less affected by water currents than by those in the air. Progress was steady.

Both rowers looked over their shoulders frequently to see whether the low clouds, colored by nitrogen dioxide, were appreciably closer, but neither allowed their efforts at the sweeps to slacken, and gradually the shore grew clearer through the haze. The Blue Hills could still be seen to the south, which was a hopeful sign. Real storms, complete with rain and wind, were usually preceded by clouds down to the surface. This fact helped Kahvi to keep her hopes up; Earrin could not keep memory of the frequent exceptions to it out of his mind.

Bones, under water fifty meters ahead, was giving no particular thought to the weather. Neither was the raft's other occupant, playing quietly with her toys in the air tent and looking up every little while to see whether her parents were doing anything new. The transparent tissue of the tent let her see them clearly enough, though the two thicknesses of it between them rather blurred the adults' view of each other.

Danna had never in her memory been this far from shore, but was quite used to having the floats tossed even more violently than they were now, so she saw no reason to be afraid. Unless she was told to put on breathing gear, she would assume that everything was all right with the raft—and even then she would probably suppose it was only a drill. She was well along in acquiring the hangups needed for survival as a Nomad. She already knew how to check the bubbles of transparent tissue in which the Sparrel pseudolife produced breathing oxygen. She could even be trusted to warn her parents if the rise in tent pressure indicated that cartridge material was becoming saturated, though she had not been trusted with the delicate task of bleeding off excess air. She was not, of course, strong enough to bring buckets of nitrogen under the raft to restore the tent's breathing balance.

She did, however, know smoke when she saw it, and it was Danna who called her parents' attention to what lay ahead. Her voice came clearly through the tent tissue as the rafts drew within three hundred meters of the Canton shore.

"Mother! Dad! Isn't that a fire on the other side of the hill? The clouds are going up, so something must be hot!"

Her elders stopped rowing and sprang to their feet, drawing the sweeps inboard by habit. They had been watching their goal, but had not looked carefully at the darkness above it. Neither could see very clearly at that distance; their mask windows were of salvaged window glass, and their eyes middle-aged. Even after the child called the smoke to their attention, it was hard for them to be sure that it was not ordinary rain scud. The ubiquitous oxides of nitrogen could be found in both.

"She's right," Kahvi said at last. "There is a fire beyond the slope. What are those Hillers doing?"

"Maybe." Earrin was less certain. "Let's see what Bones can make of it. He has decent eyesight." The man strode across the floats to the nearer of the tow lines and gave it a quick double pull. Both ropes became slack at once, and a moment later the native, as the Fyns regarded the being, surfaced a few meters away. Kahvi gave the come-here gesture, and the child imitated her,

though Bones would have had some trouble seeing her inside the tent. The creature plunged
toward the raft in a series of dolphin-like leaps,
the last of which carried its grotesque figure
smoothly to the deck. For a moment it lay like a
stranded fish; then the slender body curled upward until it stood erect, towering well above the
human beings.

The float supporting its hundred and twenty
kilograms rocked irregularly in the chop, but the
four lower limbs flexed to keep the body upright
in spite of their fantastic slenderness and appar-
ent frailty. Two of them framed the horizontal
flukes which were used in dolphin-style swimming; the other two originated half a meter
farther up the slender trunk and extended far
enough sideways and forward to provide a
trapezoidal support area quite large enough to
make balance easy. From a little distance, where
the tentacles were not noticeable, Bones would
have looked absurdly like a fish standing on its
tail, to anyone who had ever seen a fish. Kahvi and
Earrin had not; their own species was the only
macroscopic form of native animal life still surviving on Earth.

The upper handling tentacles gestured a question, and Kahvi pointed in answer.

"Fire, we think," Earrin supplemented in the
regular mix of voice and gesture. "You see better
than we. It's smoke, isn't it?"

"Yes," a tentacle signified.

"Do you remember what was growing on the
other side, there? It is explosive? Should we go
closer, or stay here, or go back?"

"Not explosive, as I recall," the Watcher signalled, "but of course it's weeks since we were here. New things could have grown, especially with those Young Ones around."

"Do you really think they'd have that much influence? The normal Hiller would destroy anything that hadn't been growing in the neighborhood for a hundred years."

"If they saw it in time," her husband pointed out. "Something could have gotten ahead of them. But that doesn't answer the question—should we risk getting closer, or wait until it burns out?"

"It's safe enough to approach, I judge," replied Bones' tentacles—the being had neither voice nor breathing equipment. "The floats are well varnished, and the tent tissue does not burn too easily. What growth I see on this side of the hill is mostly low-power, though there are a few blasters, of course."

"Are you sure?" asked Kahvi. "It looks to me as though nearly everything has become a shade lighter since we were last here. Couldn't there be overgrowth? Or have you seen this before, too?"

"No. You are right. There *is* overgrowth. I must withdraw my assurance of safety for the raft."

"And for the jail," Earrin pointed out. "If fire gets there, we'd have to walk quite a distance to the next nearest air supply. I say it's safer to get in there and clear risky plants away from the walls, if we can make it before the fire gets to this side of the hill."

"I see no people near the jail," Bones commented. "There might really be none, or they might be inside and not have seen the smoke yet,

or all be across the hill fighting the fire already. I
agree; it will be safest to protect the jail even at
some risk to the raft. It would take little to unroof
that structure."

Without further gesture the streamlined form
plunged back into the water, and a moment later
the tow lines drew taut again.

Inside the tent, Danna was looking hopefully at
her parents. She understood most of the gesture-
speech, but had evidently missed some of what
had just been said. Catching her father's eye, she
picked up her own breathing kit and made an
inquiring gesture. The parents looked at each
other and nodded, Dana's happy grin disappeared
behind her mask.

Kahvi and her husband resumed rowing, but
both kept more attention on the child than on
their goal for the next few minutes. Danna had
been carefully brought up, but they would not
have allowed her to get dressed for outdoors un-
supervised any more than either of them would
have allowed the other to do so.

The little one finished donning the acid-tight
shorts, halter, and face mask. She slung the oxygen and absorber cartridges between her narrow
shoulders, stood up, and turned slowly around for
inspection. Not until both parents had nodded
approval did she step to the space where a float
had been omitted from the deck structure, and
slip into the water.

Both parents counted subvocally, but long before the twelve seconds which would have jus-

tified action had passed the five-year-old's head showed through the other opening in the deck. She slid out of the water as smoothly as Bones; she had been swimming since before she could walk.

"Did Bones say it was a real fire?" The child was speaking as soon as her head was out of water. She used more words and fewer gestures than her parents, since her voice penetrated the mask better. "It must be big. Why are we going closer? Can I row too?"

"Bones doesn't know what's burning, but it is a big fire," replied her mother. "It may be dangerous, but we have to go close enough to save the jail—the air place on shore—in case the fire gets close to it. It will help if you row, but you must stay here when we get to shore. You'll have to take care of the raft and the tent, in case any sparks—little pieces of fire—fall on them. You have buckets ready and spill them on any fire that comes. If it doesn't come, it will be good to spill them on the tent anyway; if it's wet the fire won't hurt it. All right?"

"Sure." Danna picked up her small oar, went to her regular rowing station, and began to pull. It was doubtful whether Bones could feel the effect, but she put enough strain on the oar to feel useful.

The wind still held off, but as they approached the shore smoke came drifting to meet the raft. Danna looked over her shoulder at it occasionally, and Kahvi could see that the child was uneasy. Neither adult, however, felt seriously concerned as long as the fire itself could not be seen, and their calmness kept the little one from panic, though she had been told so much about the dangers of fire.

Fifty meters from shore Bones' form appeared, rearing up from the water and evidently standing on the bottom. The lines were still taut, but the human beings took the hint and stopped rowing. The raft could not be brought ashore, since there had to be swimming space under it to enter and leave the tent. Bones had no need for air, but had been with them since before Danna's birth and knew some of their physical requirements. One of the great eyes rolled back at the raft, while the other continued to watch the smoke, much heavier now, as it continued to jet upward from beyond the low ridge two hundred meters away.

There had been no explosions, but this was only mildly encouraging. Many plants contained both reducing tissue and nitrates, arranged with varying degrees of intimacy. They burned with varying rates when something did light them; the nitrogen real-life mutated so frequently and grew so rapidly that one could never be sure just what an apparently familiar type would do. Pseudolife was far more reliable, but there was little of that in sight.

"Nothing I can see is burning," Danna said after looking carefully. "Do you think the fire will really come over this way?"

"We can't be sure, so we'll have to watch," her father answered. "Your mother and Bones and I will all have to go ashore as soon as we're anchored to clear plants away from the jail or do whatever else is needed to keep it from losing its roof—stone won't burn, you know. You'll have to take care of home, here." The child nodded, and tried to put on a firm expression under her mask.

Bones had pulled the raft in almost to the proper depth, and now gestured that the anchors should be dropped. The adults went aft, and each lowered one of the tent-tissue sacks of boulders into the water. Danna tried to get the bow anchor overboard, but its hundred kilogram weight was far too much for her. Bones took a step toward the raft and eased the bag off the float; the child plunged in after it and swam along as it was borne a dozen meters shoreward and set firmly on the muddy bottom. Then Bones plunged back past the raft and positioned each of the other anchors in turn, the human beings paying out enough line to allow for the tide. Danna remained in the water trying to help until this job was finished; then a green-and-brown tentacle curled about her waist and lifted her, laughing, back to the deck beside her parents. They joined in the laughter for a moment, and then reached for the tools stacked beside the air tent.

"Get the buckets and keep the tent wet," the mother repeated. "We'll be able to hear you if you need us, and will watch, so don't be afraid." Kahvi plunged from the bow carrying a hoe-like implement of wood and glass. Her husband followed with a long pole carrying a sponge at the end. Bones was already halfway to the beach. The others had no chance of catching up with the creature either swimming or running, but in a meter

or so of water—too shallow for Bones to swim, too
deep for the tentacular legs to work freely—they
gained, and were close behind by the time they too
had to wade.

The beach was slimy with nitro-life, which was
(they hoped) too wet to be a fire hazard, but made
running difficult. The larger growths were mostly
of the smoldering type as far as they could see, but
there was an occasional blaster among them.

As the party reached the base of the little peninsula to the south of their anchorage, with the jail
some forty meters ahead and inland, there came a
thud which was felt rather than heard. A fountain
of red-hot coals rose into view from the other side
of the ridge, spread slowly with eye-arresting
slowness, and descended again. Some of the glowing fragments landed quite close to the watchers
and even closer to the building, and any doubts
about the nature of the bushes were quelled as
half a dozen of them, struck by the coals, began to
smoke and glow. There was no flame, since there
was practically no free oxygen to react with the
gases being distilled from the plant tissues; the
latter burned at all only because of their nitrate
content.

The human couple paused and glanced at each
other, but Bones kept running toward the jail.
After a moment they followed, but both kept
glancing quickly to the fire, back to the raft, and
forward to the stone structure, while staying as
far as possible from any bushes close to their path.

The native had almost reached the building,
with the others eight or ten meters behind, when

there was a second, heavier explosion. All three stopped to watch the glowing fragments of stems, trunks, and branches fly upward and outward, each trailing a line of red-brown nitrogen dioxide smoke and gas. They tensed as some of the material passed over their heads, and Earrin and Kahvi held their breaths as several incandescent fragments fell into the water on both sides of the raft. Kahvi took a step back the way they had come, but stopped as she saw her daughter's tiny form stand firm between two water buckets. Evidently nothing had hit the tent this time.

Then a scream, in a voice much deeper than Danna's, turned their attention back toward the jail.

JANET AULISIO

II

Cooling, Carefully

The building had walls of rough stone, with no visible mortar. The cement which held it together was as flammable as ordinary tent tissue, but had been applied only to the inside of the walls; it was safe from outside fire unless one of the more flammable varieties of slime were allowed to grow on the stones. The roof, however, was another matter. It had to be transparent to let sunlight reach the oxygen plants inside. Unless some change had been made since the Fyns' last visit, it was composed of the same material as their own tent on the raft, and their other bases. It was not actually explosive, but vulnerable to fire when dry.

The scream seemed to suggest that there had been no change, not a surprising situation for the Boston area.

Earrin dashed up to the building; he did not need Bones' gesture to tell him the cause of the outcry, though only the Observer was tall enough to see all the roof. The man climbed the wall without difficulty, using the ample toe-spaces between the stones. His sponge was already wet.

There were three widening holes in the roof, smoking briskly around their edges. Earrin got as close as he could to the nearest, reached out with his pole, and began sponging its rim. It was tempting to move the pole too fast, but nitrate-fed fires were not smothered; they had to be cooled. Earrin had had far too much experience to let himself be rushed on this job.

This did not seen to be true of the person inside. There had been no more screams, which was encouraging—perhaps the first had been mere surprise, not panic. Now a sponge was dabbing at the second hole from underneath—but it *was* going too fast; the widening rim of the opening resumed its hissing and smoking as the sponge passed on.

"Slow down!" Earrin cried as loudly as his mask would allow. "You're not getting it out!"

A less muffled male voice responded. "But there's more than one! If I don't go fast, the others will get too big!"

Earrin was startled by this logic, but attacked

from another direction. "We'll get the others. You stick with that one, and slow down." His use of the plural had been slightly deceptive, he suddenly realized, since neither Bones nor Kahvi had sponges, but there was no time to make amends for the moral slip. At least it had been effective; the occupant of the jail followed instructions. Earrin finished the hole he had started, and leaped along the wall to the remaining one. At the same moment another explosion sounded, but he kept his attention on his job. Kahvi and Bones would warn him if any other action was necessary. He wished they had more sponges, but there had been no way of telling before they left the raft just what would be needed; it had been at least as likely that they would have to be hoeing firebreaks around the jail. One thing did occur to him as he moved, and he called out, "Kahvi! Bones! There's at least one more sponge inside. Check there before you go back to the raft for anything!"

"Right," his wife responded. "That last blast was weaker, and nothing got this far. If I go inside I'll let you know so you can watch the raft. Danna can't handle that much by herself."

"Right." Earrin had reached the last hole, and was working on it. It had had time to grow large, over twenty centimeters across, and the sponge might not be enough, but one could only try.

The near edge of the sputtering circle sizzled more loudly as the still-wet tool drank its heat. Earrin moved it along as fast as he dared. The sponge itself was only a dozen centimeters across—it would be nice, he thought fleetingly, if

larger ones could be found, but the pseudolife
which produced the things had apparently been
designed for some long-forgotten purpose that
needed small sponges. At least it was still holding
plenty of water.

By the time he was halfway around the hole, it
was evident that geometry was against him.
Without stopping his own efforts, the man called
out, "Bones! Knife work!"

The hole was near one corner of the roof, not
quite a meter from the south and west walls. The
Observer was tall enough to see the situation
without climbing, and the tentacles which extended from just below the bulging eyes were
more than long enough. One of them slipped the
glass-bladed knife from Earrin's pouch and began
sawing at the rim of the hole. The blade was not
really knifelike by earlier standards—it would
have done better as one half of a pair of scissors—
but the tissue gave easily under its attack. Bones
started on the side where the fire was already out,
slashed outward, and then began to saw
clockwise. A strip of separated material began to
hang down into the room, and started to flame in
the breathable air inside. Bones worked faster,
and got the strip separated before it had ignited
more of the roof; the flaming stuff dropped out of
sight inside. Earrin held his sponge ready for several seconds, but luck had apparently been with
them.

"All right, Kahv," he finally called. "We got
two, the fellow inside put out the other. Can you
see if Dan's all right? This mask window is terrible."

"I can see her pretty well. She's just standing there, and there's no smoke, so I guess the raft wasn't hit. I'll go back and make sure, and get another sponge; we won't need a fire break, I'd say. You and Bones stay here—the fire over the hill is still going, judging by the smoke there."

"Maybe it would be better for Bones to go back," Earrin pointed out. "He can travel faster, and it would be better for you to talk to this fellow inside."

"All right," the woman agreed. "Bones—" she shifted from mostly voice to mostly gesture. The fishlike being waved agreement with an upper tentacle and moved away, the strangely rigid walking tendrils moving almost invisibly fast. Another explosion took the human beings' attention from raft and messenger for a moment, but again nothing fell dangerously close to either structure.

"I don't see how this can last much longer," Earrin remarked. "It's strange that the smoke is all coming up from one spot, as though the initial fire weren't spreading. How could it have so much fuel in one spot?"

"You stay up there and watch. I'll go in and see if the jailbird knows anything about it," Kahvi suggested. Earrin glanced downward. The transparent roof tissue reflected enough sky light to prevent a clear view of what was under it, but he could make out some movement.

"Wait a minute," he said. "I think someone's coming out. He has a mask on, anyway."

"How can he do that? Has he fixed the roof already?"

"No. Maybe—" Earrin fell silent; he could think
of no possible reason for letting roof repair drop
from top priority. "Maybe you'd better go in, at
that," he said at last. "I'll watch." Neither of them
was suspicious by nature, but there was something strange here.

Kahvi was already heading for the air lock, a
pool of water extending under the east wall. Her
husband watched her submerge and, with more
difficulty, saw her emerge inside the building.
With difficulty, he reminded himself firmly that
his current job was fire watch; but he still glanced
downward occasionally.

Kahvi straightened up—the pool was less than a
meter and a half deep under the wall—and went
up the steps to the floor level. They had been here
before many times, and a quick glance showed
little general change. Her main interest was in the
room's single occupant.

This was a man—really little more than an ado-
lescent, years younger than either Kahvi or Earrin, much thinner than even the latter, and several
centimeters taller than either of the Fyns. He was
even thinner than the typical Hiller, and his skin
shed no trace of the yellow characteristic of
people who spent much time outdoors. The
hundredth-normal nitric acid of the oceans was
too dilute to color proteins, but the rain was sometimes another matter. His hair looked a little too
long for comfortable mask work. The woman took
in all this at the first glance, while stepping
quickly toward the wall opposite the lock.

"Why don't you fix your roof?" she snapped as

she threaded her way among the tables covered with oxygen plants.

The boy swept off the mask he had been adjusting.

"I was going to. What's the rush?"

"You're letting oxygen out, and spores in. Here are your patches. Here's the cement. Get that small hole at the north end—I can't reach it. I'll work on that big one over the table—you idiot! One of the trays on that table is burning! Toss it into the lock, clean it out, finish patching these holes, and then get it restocked. I suppose some stuff from the roof fell on it. Move! If you're here for education, it doesn't seem to be taking!"

The youngster's face flushed, but he made no answer. He moved at about half Kahvi's speed to the indicated table, picked up the tray of psuedolife which was flaming in the rich atmosphere, and carried it to the air lock. The fire had started in the middle of the half-meter-square box, and had not yet come close enough to the edges to make them impossible to handle; but he winced as the flames and smoke curled upward from his burden, and held it as far from himself as his strength allowed. Kahvi noted that he also held it away from the other tables, so perhaps he was somewhere above the moron level—when she was annoyed, she sometimes didn't distinguish carefully between stupidity and the ignorance which could, after all, be equally deadly.

She leaped to the table where the burning tray had been, and reached up with the patch she had been cementing as she crossed the room. The roof was still somewhat out of reach, but a jump put her high enough to slap the square of tissue against the hole. The cement would hold it in place for the few hours it would need to grow into union with the rest of the roof. This was the largest hole, the one her husband and Bones had extinguished last. The others were not directly over tables, but with a wordless gesture she directed the jailbird to move two of the latter. Within two more minutes the roof was airtight, and she descended from the last table to face the young Hiller.

"All right, I'm sorry I was insulting," she said after eyeing him silently for a moment. "I suppose there's some reason why I found you fumbling with a mask as though you were going outside, instead of fixing your roof."

"I was going out to help put out fires on the roof," he replied. "Suppose a whole lot of sparks had come at once?"

"Suppose they had. You had a sponge and water in here, and could work just as well with them as Earrin could from on top—better; you could wet your sponge more easily. There were no patches outside, and a hole needs to be patched as soon as possible. Didn't anyone teach you that before they sent you here?"

"Of course." The voice and expression were sullen, now. "I'd have done the patching when no more fire arrived. Putting that out came first, it seemed to me."

"True enough, but someone else was taking care of that, and as I said you could do it better from inside. Were you trying to *think*?"

"Of course. If you don't think before you act, you can kill people. Everyone knows that—or weren't *you* taught anything?"

"Lots. Thinking may be all right inside a city, but outdoors or as near to outdoors are we are here, you don't let thinking interfere with your hangups. Thinking is too slow to keep you alive. If you don't have the right habits, then hoping is better than—grab a sponge! Here's some more!" Two almost simultaneous thuds had sounded.

There were several of the sponge-tipped rods lying against the walls; Kahvi seized one as she spoke. Simultaneously her husband's voice sounded from above. "Kahv! More fire! I'll take the east wall, where I can wet my sponge in the lock pool!"

Kahvi tore off her mask to permit freer speech and shouted her agreement. For the next few seconds she paid no attention to the jailbird, but he also seized a rod with commendable speed, and a moment later they were far too busy to exchange anything but brief gestures as a dozen sputtering coals landed on the roof. None of the resulting holes burned wider than sponge size before being chilled into quiescence, but patches were still being applied when the next explosion sounded. For a quarter of an hour everyone was too occupied to think, though in one brief lull Kahvi called up to her husband, "What about the raft? Is Danna all right?" She did not allow her concern to interfere with her activity.

"I can't see very well," Earrin reminded her. "There doesn't seem to be any smoke out that way, though, and Bones hasn't come back." He suggested no reasons for the latter fact; Kahvi could make appropriate inferences for herself. If either parent was worried, however, it didn't show while the work went on.

Eventually the smoke from beyond the ridge thinned and died, and the frightening thuds of exploding wood ceased to sound. The roof of the jail was a mass of patches, but it was airtight.

"I think we're through with it," Earrin called. "I'll stay up here for a while, though. You can relax inside."

"What about the others?" Kahvi asked.

"All right, I'm sure. The raft is there and looks all right—one of us is going to have to make me a better mask. Maybe if the Hillers don't need all this shipment—yes, I can see them both coming this way, now. Danna's in front, and she'd be hanging back if anything much had happened to the raft or the tent, since we told her to take care of them."

"Glass? Raft? You must be the traders," the occupant of the jail cut in. "No wonder you were so full of outside customs. I should have thought. I must have lost track of the days—you weren't due for a week yet, were you?"

"They said two months, which would be the middle of May. I don't know the exact date—we always seem to get out of step by a day or two— but I don't think we're that far off," the woman said. "How long have you been here? Have they kept you completely out of touch? That's pretty stiff."

"I'm not a jailbird. I'm doing a job, not serving a

sentence. I was supposed to be ready for you—they told me by the middle of June. O'Donohugh must have—hmm. I think I know what happened. You'd better have your friends come inside. I do hope you can live through this."

III

Morals, Mostly

Kahvi felt better. The words were not encouraging, but the young fellow seemed to have some of the courtesy reflexes.

"Thanks," she replied. "There was no need to have anyone waiting especially for us, though; we could have gone up to the Hill to let you know we were here."

"Well, we wanted to know as soon as possible. There are—or maybe *were*—some projects going on here in Canton and we were using this building a lot anyway. I hope you brought as much glass as we asked for; it's badly needed—or was."

"Was needed? Had projects? What's changed? And what were the projects? Why did they need so much glass—if you want to tell, of course."

"Well, I'm not really sure about the past tense, but the fire you just helped fight off seems to have started very close to where we had things going. Whether anything is left I'll have to find out. I *hope* we can still use your cargo."

"And that you can still pay for it," added Kahvi. "We can take credit, of course; it's always nice to have someone who owes us air."

"That's right, there are two of you, aren't there—your partner is still up on the roof. I suppose you'll need help in getting the cargo ashore. Should I come now? Or wait—you mentioned other names. Has your group gotten larger?"

"Not really." Kahvi began to feel a little tense, and wondered whether he were making some reference to her figure. "It's been the same group for years, but usually Earrin and I are the only ones to trade. This time the cargo is bigger and the raft harder to move. We don't really need help in unloading, and you'll have to restock your air tray anyway before you come out, of course. It was very lucky that only one coal landed in an oxygen tray, wasn't it?" Kahvi had just realized how incredibly lucky this was, and was wondering how it had been possible to save the roof at all.

If the boy read anything into her remark, however, his expression showed no sign of it. Kahvi felt her own skin flush, and deliberately slowed her breathing. "We'll go back and start unloading now, as long as you're all right here," she went on as calmly as she could. "Where did I put my mask? There—thanks. You'd better fix that tray, and do something about patching tissue. We've used up three quarters of what you had."

"No hurry about that," was the reply. "There's no way we can have another fire for a while—oh, sorry; that's another Nomad must-do, isn't it? Well, maybe you're right. I'll take care of them both before I come out to help. Maybe you could bring some glass here right away; I don't have anything smooth enough to grow good patch tissue on."

"All right." The woman had redonned her mask by this time, but still used spoken words. The Hiller would not understand Nomad gesture speech, still less the symbols used by the Fyn family and Bones. "One of us will be back in a few minutes. Do you want some help with nitrogen, too?"

She regretted this question the instant it was uttered, and glanced up at her husband. She could see him clearly enough but knew that he could not see her nearly as well through the reflecting roof tissue, and for a moment she felt a twinge of fear. However, the young Bostonian seemed indifferent to any implications in her remark, and a moment later she was through the air lock.

She looked up again at Earrin, and gestured him to come with her back toward the raft. Danna and Bones were now only a few meters away, and she repeated the signal to them. Her husband glanced toward the spot from which the smoke no longer rose, shrugged, and made his way down the wall. The party was halfway back to the raft before Kahvi said anything.

"Could you hear him?" she asked her husband.

"Not very well. You seemed to be schoolmarming at first."

"I was. I'm not sure what we should be doing about him."

"Why anything? What's wrong with him? What's his name, and why is he there?"

"He said he wasn't a jailbird, but I don't believe him. He's a junky—a waster. There isn't a nitrogen plant or intake tube in the place. Why the roof didn't go up in one big flare I can't see, and I'm still dizzy from the oxygen—he's got a full atmosphere of it in there. He wants glass to grow patch sheets on, and I suppose we'd better give it to him, but we'll have to stay on the raft ourselves—that jail is no place for Danna."

"What's his name?"

"I didn't get it."

"Then he'll know you spotted something wrong." Kahvi nodded slowly. Exchange of names was another of the life-protecting habits of the nomadic people outside the cities. Without that information one could not talk about another person to a third party without ambiguity, and precise communication was one of the necessities of life. The same factor underlay the Nomad abhorrence of lying. Kahvi's failure to ask for the jailbird's name would make it obvious that she was being disturbed or distracted by something.

"He must know anyway," she said finally. "I did say something about his shortage of N-gear. Earrin, what should we do? Of course we have to give him the life-support stuff he needs, but I'm afraid of him. He doesn't care about rules—I don't know what he's likely to do."

"I'll bring him the glass," replied the man. "Don't worry about that. Maybe this will help, in a way. We can let Bones help with the unloading; if this fellow does see him, no one is likely to believe him anyway. It probably wouldn't even matter if he saw Danna."

"I don't think we should take that chance. They'd grab her for Surplus school and think they were doing her and us a favor. You know that as well as I do. Look, this junky spoke about a project where the fire was, and if he wasn't dreaming there are probably other people over there, which is much too close. They might be over any minute to see what happened to their jail, and if *they* see Bones or Danna—well, they can't all be oxygen-freaks."

Earrin nodded. "You're right. They'd better get out of sight." He gestured briefly to Bones, and the native disappeared without a splash into the water. Danna followed, unwillingly. She didn't want to go back inside the tent, but was well enough brought up to know when things were necessary. She gave a reproachful look at her father's gesture, and disappeared as smoothly as her nonhuman friend. A minute or so later her head appeared briefly inside the tent, signifying her safe arrival; then she dropped out of sight among the bubble-covered trays of air producers and food plants. Her parents saw, but devoted most of their

attention to the ridge for several more minutes.
Finally, however, they decided that there had
been no witnesses to the presence of child or native, and went to work on the cargo.

The copper was in sacks similar to the anchors,
each containing twenty of the two-kilogram
nuggets brought ashore by the pseudoliving
metal-collecting robots which still bred and operated in the oceans. The change in Earth's air had
been much harder on natural life than on the
artificial varieties. Fifteen of the sacks were on the
raft. Kahvi dropped each in turn into the meter-
deep acid, and her husband carried them ashore,
not lifting them above the surface until it was
unavoidable. Bones moved some of them as close
to shore as possible without appearing above the
surface.

The glass, similarly wrapped, consisted of
whole window panes salvaged from the harbor
bottom by the native. Vast numbers of these still
lay where they had settled into the mud as the
houses disintegrated around them. There had
only been enough oxygen in Earth's atmosphere
to make the oceans about one-hundredth-normal
in nitric acid as it combined with the nitrogen, but
rain, rivers, and even estuaries had often been
much more concentrated during the fix. Metals in
general were now completely dissolved, except
for the nuggets which the pseudoliving collectors
were still reducing in their mindless way. Glass
and ceramics, of course, could still be found.

By the time the last of the cargo was above high
water mark the sun was low in the west. The

jailbird had not reappeared, and if there had been any Hillers at the fire site they had shown no interest in the jail side of the ridge. There had been no more smoke, and no sounds, from that direction.

Kahvi, who had helped carry material ashore as soon as everything was off the deck, straightened up and stretched. Then she looked at the jail and frowned slightly.

"He never came out, did he?" she commented. "I wonder what he's doing in there. He's had plenty of time to fix that oxygen tray."

"I'll bring him some glass," Earrin answered the unspoken thought. "I want to see what he's like, anyway."

"I'm afraid of him," Kahvi admitted. "I'll go along and watch from the roof. If he tries to do anything to you I can threaten to cut it open."

Earrin raised his acid-yellowed eyebrows. "I know you love me, but that's going pretty far. He probably wouldn't believe you could do it, any more than I do. Besides, you've been working pretty hard, and Dan's been alone quite a while. You go eat and rest, and make her happy for a while. You do have other responsibilities besides me."

"I know, but I don't always want to remember them."

"Sorry, dearest. I can look after myself this time, I think. Would you say this character is any stronger than I am? Was there anything he could use for a weapon?"

"I don't suppose he's as strong as either of us

normally, but if he's breathing straight oxygen there's no telling what he can do. Anything that can be picked up can be a weapon, I've heard. I'm just afraid of him; he doesn't think rules are for him, so there's no telling what he'd do."

"All right. I'm not afraid of him yet, but I may be after I've seen and talked to him, and I'll be careful anyway. Tell you what—I'll tell Bones what I'm doing. He'll want to watch, since the jailbird is something new. He'll help if the fellow tries to do anything to me."

"Are you sure? He may just go on watching. That'll be something new for him, too, remember. Besides, what if other Hillers come and see her? We can't afford to let them know we associate with natives."

"Why should they suppose we're associating? Natives are always watching things—even Hillers must know that."

Kahvi frowned in thought for several seconds. She ran her fingers through her short, acid-yellowed hair where it was not covered by mask straps, and her dark brown eyes looked searchingly into Earrin's blue ones. "All right," she said at last, "but get back as quickly as you can, please. I suppose I did promise him the glass." She turned away and started to wade toward the raft. "I'll tell Bones. She's probably under the raft playing with Dan. Don't go in until she's with you." Earrin nodded, and picked up one of the bundles of glass panes. He was no longer even amused at his wife's choice of pronouns when referring to Bones; neither of them knew which gender, if either, was appropriate. His use of masculine and hers of feminine had been mostly a joke when it first started; now it was merely habit. If Bones noticed the difference in language, the Watcher had never commented about it.

The brassy patch in the sky which marked the sun's position was almost against the hill which had concealed the fire, as Earrin approached the jail again. He glanced behind him as he reached the air lock pool, and saw Bones' bulk surface briefly with one huge eye turned shoreward. Kahvi had passed the word. He turned back to the building.

"This is Earrin Fyn the Nomad," he called loudly. "I'm bringing the glass Kahvi promised. May I come in?"

"I'll be glad to see you, Nomad Fyn. Come along." There had been no hesitation in the answer, and no suggestion of surprise in the speaker's voice; if anything, it was more of a bored drawl. Earrin turned once more, signalled briefly to the partly visible native, and lowered himself and his burden into the pool.

Kahvi had described the man, so the centimeters of extra height and kilograms of lacking weight were no surprise to Earrin. As the woman had said, the jailbird's hair was long enough to suggest that outdoor attire was not usual for him, and dark enough to indicate little if any exposure to nitric acid rain. A glance around the room confirmed the other point; there were three different types of photosynthetic oxygen producers among the trays, all of them pseudolife, but neither plant nor tubing to provide free nitrogen. Several hoses did reach through the air lock, but their inner ends entered tanks in which pseudolife forms precipitated carbon dioxide as calcium carbonate—they simply provided fertilizer for the oxygen-makers. Earrin could not detect the excess oxygen by smell, of course, but since the total pressure must be about the same inside as out—the roof tissue was neither bulging nor sagging—there could be no doubt about what they were breathing. The Nomad deliberately slowed and shallowed his respiration, and hoped he wasn't being obvious about it. He had removed his mask from habit as he emerged from the pool, and hoped he had suppressed all signs of the urge to clap it back on as he realized what the air inside must be.

If there had been any such faux pas, the Hiller seemed not to notice it.

"Thanks for the glass," he said. "It was foolish of me to tell your partner that it should be a long time before I'd need any patch material. There is never any way to be sure, is there? I hope I didn't shock her too much. You Nomads are very sensitive about what's right and what's wrong, aren't you?"

"Being wrong is very often being dead," Earrin pointed out. "Kahvi and I have travelled enough, though, to know that what is right outdoors may not always be so in a city. We hope she didn't offend."

"Not at all," the boy assured him. "I do know that mere customs aren't necessarily right. Most of my fellow citizens, as you must have noticed on your earlier visits, are a bit reluctant to accept or adopt anything new, but I and some of my friends don't feel that way at all. That's why we wanted your metal and glass."

"Even the others aren't completely down on new things," Earrin pointed out. "I remember occasionally selling them a new product, and we are still eating from a pseudo plant which was developed here."

"By a friend of mine, who is very unpopular with the fogies as a result," the other assured him. "As a Nomad yourself, if you'll forgive my mentioning it, you presumably don't mind new things."

"Of course not. They're most of my living. Are you suggesting you have something we might like?"

"I got the impression that you and your wife had both noticed it already."

"You mean—but—" Earrin found himself at a loss for words. The jailbird smiled.

"Not quite as open-minded as you like to think. I'm not really trying to change your life-style, but didn't you wonder under the circumstances why my roof didn't burn far more violently?"

Earrin kicked himself mentally. "Yes," he admitted, "we did wonder about that. You have a new roof tissue, then? We certainly would be interested—unless—" he paused again. The other laughed rather bitterly.

"Unless it needs straight oxygen to grow in?"

"That thought did occur."

"I have to admit I don't know. It hasn't been

tried under your—uh—rather dull environmental conditions. I could let you have some for testing, with the understanding that you would be in my debt if results were satisfactory."

"That's all right. When you have a replacement supply, I'll bring a sheet or two more glass—"

"You needn't wait that long. I'll give you a sample now, if you'll help me seed the glass you just brought. I suppose it will shock you as it did your companion, but I'm really not in a state of panic about replacing my roofing. The city, not to mention a good many other air stations, is well within walking distance, you know. I hope you're not too unsettled by my attitude."

"Well—I suppose when you live in a city, less closely connected with your air supply than a Nomad or a Surplus kid, you'd feel a little different about such things. I admit that taking something so necessary from you when your own supply is so short seems very wrong—but if you really want it that way—I mean—if you're—" Earrin ran out of words again. The Hiller laughed, and for a moment even Kahvi, had she seen his face, might not have been afraid of him.

"If I'm not out of my mind, you mean?"

"Well—not exactly—but under the circumstances—"

"Come on, fellow. Just because I like to breathe natural air that's worth putting in your lungs, instead of that diluted stuff you put up with, doesn't mean my brain's burned out. I suppose that's what you're thinking, isn't it?"

"Not exactly. There's nothing natural about

this stuff, and right now I'm not quite sure what I'm thinking. I feel a little strange."

"Well, let's get it over with. Unpack your glass and I'll cut up some of the patches. You can help me apply them, and you'll be outside again in a few minutes. If you're really uncomfortable, why don't you put your mask back on?"

"Indoors? But that's not—I mean—"

"I know. It's not right to use an air cartridge when you can breathe without it. Well, if you're stuck with your own habits, you're stuck with 'em. Would you rather we talked outside?"

"Yes." Earrin answered almost without thought, then flushed. The other began donning his mask without comment, though his face was expressive until the breathing gear hid it, and Fyn waited silently until he had finished. Then the Hiller started down the steps into the air lock.

The Nomad waited until his surprisingly accommodating host had ducked below the surface, then began to follow him into the water.

He got down only three steps. Then, without warning, there came a firm grip on his ankle, and his footing was pulled from under him. He fell heavily backward; his skull met the edge of one of the plant tables, and he did not feel the floor.

JANET AULISIO

IV

Unknown, Unless

Bones, almost frantic with excitement, was completely happy. Two areas of Unknown competed for the attention of the strange mind and senses. A human being of the hunting-and-gathering era would have felt much the same if he had been placed in possession of an indefinitely large food supply, with his only choice that of what to eat first. Adolescents from the mechanized Age of Pleasure, much later, had the same difficulty.

Sex was unknown to the Observer, and eating no particular pleasure. The fishlike body did pos-

41

sess a sense of taste, but selecting diet items with its aid was not even a minor intellectual problem—just a matter of being sure to consume equivalent amounts of oxidizing and reducing foods. The only real fun came in learning whether a particular food item was still the same this time as it had been before; the nitrogen real-life duplicated itself rather unreliably, and mutations were the rule rather than the exception.

The present situation, on the other hand, was really enthralling. The human Earrin had gone into the jail where there seemed to be another of his species. Could they really transfer memories only by this crude sound-and-gesture code? Bones wasn't yet quite sure. He had suspected Earrin and Kahvi of using more natural methods, but they preferred to be alone at such times and details were lacking.

A few hundred meters away on the other side of the hill was the area which had just been burning. What had started the fire? What had furnished the fuel? Had it stopped merely because there was nothing else to burn, or had more human beings been involved? Bones had seen the region before, but nothing in memory offered answers to these questions. Like the jail, the far side of the hill was a blank on the knowledge map. The only real emotional drive Bones' species knew was the urge to fill such gaps, though the desire to share the knowledge when it had been acquired could at times rise nearly as high. How to choose between two Unknowns?

The jail, of course, was closer. The fact that Bones had been asked to stay and help Earrin if need arose was not a major consideration; the Observer could see no reason why the man should need help. Hillers did seem to disapprove of Observers for some reason, but the notion that human beings might deliberately injure each other was not to be driven into Bones' consciousness for some time yet. Even Kahvi's evident uneasiness about the situation had not impressed the strange mind in that way, though it had partially faced the idea that human beings might be separate individuals rather than a group of Observer units.

The important thing was to find out, and watching Earrin and this other being seemed to offer some chance of accomplishing this end.

The Observer therefore emerged from the water moments after Fyn had gone through the air lock and approached the jail. Keeping mind that being seen by other people would be undesirable, the fishlike being kept on the east side of the building; the most likely direction of approach for other human beings was presumably the west, where the fire had been. Why no one had yet come from that direction was merely part of the other tantalizing blank which the Observer had deliberately scheduled into second priority.

Looking from the east did have a major disadvantage with the sun low in the west, but it was possible to make out the two human figures. They were obviously using the sound code—there were practically no gestures, and only an occasional word could be grasped, so there was no way of telling what thoughts were being exchanged.

Bones considered entering the air lock and ob-

serving from just below the surface inside, but
this did not really promise an improvement and
would prevent the reception of any warning of the
approach of others. Kahvi might be persuaded to
come and listen; she could translate—no, she had
clearly intended to remain with her bud for a
time. Bones' patience was comparable to that of a
stable human being, and it was therefore not un-
limited. Important as this observation was, the
temptation to do something more productive
grew stronger by the moment. Both mind and
eyes began to wander, and Bones failed to notice
when one of the human beings donned outdoor
equipment and entered the air lock. It was sound
rather than sight which attracted the Observer's
awareness to the pool a couple of meters away.

The sound was an exclamation in a human
voice, muffled as usual by a breathing mask.
Bones' nearer eye swivelled down in time to see a
head jerk back under the water. The sky was still
bright enough for reflection to obscure things
below this surface too, and for a moment the
streamlined body stood tense with indecision.
Then motion inside the building caught the other
eye.

The figure still standing alone suddenly fell,
though no reason could be seen. Another human
being emerged from the inner pool and bent over
the prostrate one, apparently removing the latter's breathing mask, though details were not
clear. This seemed interesting enough to change
priorities, and Bones entered the air lock.

There was no question of helping Earrin; there

was no question of helping anyone—Bones did not even know that Earrin was the one who had fallen, though it seemed likely. There was no question of personal violence. There was just Question, another blank area on that incredible mental map. Something was happening which did not fit any previous experience, and an explanation had to be found.

Though much taller than that of any human being, Bones' form was slender enough to get under the wall without trouble; two or three seconds sufficed to traverse the lock. The shadowy jail would have forced human eyes to delay for adaptation, but those of the Observer reacted more quickly. Even so, little information came through at first.

The person on the floor was Earrin Fyn, but what the other was doing—helping or hurting—was still not obvious. He stopped doing it instantly on perceiving the newcomer, and sprang to his feet.

His mask was off and his words unmuffled, but they meant nothing to Bones. The actions which followed did carry information, however; the Observer was clearly unwelcome. The fellow seized a meter-long sponge rod and swung it violently. Bones ducked quickly enough to save an eye, but got a painful jolt on the left jaw. The second came much lower, and its force was absorbed by the cartilaginous ribs of the broad fin which ran down the same side. Neither blow did serious damage—not nearly enough to start a budding reaction—but both hurt, and neither brought any

consolation in the form of new knowledge. Bones'
reaction was almost human, and the third swing
was stopped short of its target.

The tentacles which sprouted just below each
eye and above the lateral fins lashed out. One
seized the stick, and the other snapped whiplike
against the man's bare chest. It did not actually
break the skin, but left a red welt a centimeter
wide and ten or twelve long, and the man fell back
with a wordless shriek. Then he uttered two or
three more syllables at Bones, several others
which seemed to be directed at Fyn's still motionless body, and snatched up a breathing mask and
set of cartridges from a nearby table. He seemed
to have some trouble adjusting these; Bones had
never seen a human being in a state of panic and
was tempted to offer help, but fortunately made
no actual move before the job was done.

The fellow disappeared into the lock pool, edg-
ing around to keep out of Bones' reach as he approached it, and uttering a final burst of syllables
as he submerged. Bones was tempted to follow,
but Fyn's motionless body offered an equally attractive mystery and the Observer stayed.

In several years' companionship with the Fyn
family the Observer had learned much. Uncon-
sciousness at night and after heavy exertion was a
familiar phenomenon with these beings, but it
was unusual for it to come on this suddenly. Besides, while Fyn had been working quite hard
during the last few hours, he had shown none of
the usual preliminary symptoms, and it was not
yet quite night. The man was clearly alive; his

body was undergoing the endless inflation-deflation cycle which Bones now knew to be its oxygen-feeding mechanism. The discovery that this life form could use only gaseous oxygen, rather than nitrates, in its redox energy machinery had driven the Observer on a frantic search for another unit to which the knowledge could be transferred. It had fitted so neatly into the old hypothesis that livable planets always went through a stage when they had free oxygen in their atmospheres, before they acquired their permanent gas envelopes . . .

The Fyn family had never found out why their strange companion had disappeared for a month.

Bones had no information on which to base effective first aid for the unconscious man, and did not really help him. The lump on the back of Earrin's head was not pronounced enough to be seen by the great eyeballs or noticed by the strange, fluid nervous system which operated them. It was probably the over-oxygenated air of the jail which was the main cause of Fyn's rapid recovery, but this never occurred to Bones. A gas analysis was, from the Observer's point of view, something which could be accomplished easily enough with the appropriate physical and chemical equipment; but having no breathing equipment, the species had never evolved a sense of smell. Receptors analogous to taste buds existed on the outer skin as well as inside the mouth, and operated well enough under water, but Bones was not equipped to detect oxygen personally.

It was nearly dark when Earrin opened his eyes.

He could make out the figure of the native standing over him, but gestures could not be made out and communication was therefore limited. The man knew of course that the other had no vocal apparatus, and he and his wife had both come to realize that there was some limitation to the creature's hearing, though neither could make out just what it was. Most of the scientific knowledge still retained by humanity was chemical rather than in the more general physical sciences, and neither Earrin nor Kahvi, well-read as the latter was, knew anything of the physics of sound. An explanation, however detailed, that Bones' kind lacked both pitch and timbre discrimination would have meant nothing to either. They knew only that their strange friend seemed unable to distinguish words which seemed quite different to them, and that it was necessary to supplement vocal communication with gestures.

Even without real conversation, Bones could tell that Earrin was having trouble getting to his feet, and after a moment the tentacles helped. Earrin, confused and with no recollection of just what had happened before he had been stunned, groped in the near-darkness for his breathing gear, found and donned it, and led the way outside.

Here it was bright enough to communicate, though the sun had set. Unfortunately, Fyn had little to communicate. He tried to get across the notion of an oxygen addict, and the native was delighted with the indirect information thus provided. It now seemed well established that human beings were in fact *individuals*, genuinely incapable of direct communication. This brought up so many unthought-of implications that the Observer was almost dazed at the new Unknowns opening up. What happened to a human mind before it had learned the communication code? Earrin and Kahvi had kept the bud Danna—how had they known that it was a true copy? Two others had been produced since and had not been kept, though the units had been buried rather than eaten—why? Was there no risk from inaccurate copies? How did the human mind face the fact that nearly all the knowledge it acquired could not be transmitted and must be destroyed when the unit which had acquired it terminated its action? Psychology was an entirely new idea to a being which had hitherto known only a single mind.

Fyn, of course, was not concerned with anything abstract. He wondered where the jailbird might have gone, but there was no way to tell. The nearest place where he could have disappeared was over the ridge to the west, toward the fire site. However, the darkness showed that Earrin himself had been unconscious long enough to permit the other possibilities—northward toward the end of the Canton peninsula, or south toward the Blue Hills and the city. Kahvi might have seen him go, of course, but this seemed doubtful—in that case she would have come to learn what had happened to Earrin.

There seemed nothing to do except go back to the raft, and tell the others what had happened—Danna was included in family discussions as a matter of course.

There was no family discussion that night, however.

Bones, far taller than Fyn's one and two-thirds meters, saw the motion first and reacted instantly as had long ago been agreed with the family. The slender form vanished almost soundlessly into the sea, without giving any signal of intent or explanation. The man needed none.

The most likely direction was still westward. He looked that way, and saw six human heads rising from behind the ridge. They were clearly visible against the still bright sky; it seemed worth hoping that they had not seen Bones. However, it must be obvious to them that Fyn himself had been in or near the jail. Had the oxygen-waster gone to get them? Were they friends of that rather strange character? Earrin still had no idea what had knocked him out; maybe the fellow had gone for help. In any case, there was nothing to be done except wait and see what these Hillers wanted, and hope they asked no embarrassing questions about natives. As a Nomad, his social status with Hillers was already low enough; if they thought he were actually associating with the animals, it might make a living harder to earn.

So Fyn, still not quite to the pile of cargo they had brought ashore, stood and waited for the newcomers. When they got close enough to identify figures, it became evident that the jailbird was not among them. However, all six seemed to be in the same general age group, perhaps sixteen or seventeen. Two of them were women. It was one of these who spoke when the group came within two or three meters.

"You're the Nomad Earrin Fyn, aren't you?" she asked.

"That's right." The Hillers used only spoken words, shouted through their breathing masks, like other city dwellers. Fyn did not attempt gesture language, which was essentially a family development unknown even to other Nomads. "We brought the copper and glass you wanted," he added.

"So we see. Is this all you could get?"

"All in the time you gave us. We had to enlarge the raft to carry this, as it was. We can make more trips if you want, but you know there is nothing to be done about the rate copper comes in from the sea. Glass we can get as fast as we can pick it up."

"Where do you get it?"

Fyn's smile was concealed both by mask and darkness, but the Hillers might as well have seen it. The question was not repeated.

"Well, this will help us start over," the woman went on after a moment. "We'll certainly need more, though, so you might as well start after it as soon as you can."

"There is payment for this load." Fyn was not at all diffident about making this point.

"You'll get it. I'm afraid there is no place ashore where you can relax, however, while you wait. The jail here is no longer suitable—perhaps you have noticed."

"Yes. My wife and I have both been there. Education is not working very well, I judge."

"Did you have trouble?"

"Not exactly. My wife went first and was frightened by the situation, but not by anything he did. She promised him glass for growing patch tissue—his roof was damaged by the fire this afternoon—and I just delivered it. I gathered from what he said that the person there—I'm afraid we never got his name—is one of your group."

"True. He is." One of the young men was speaking this time. "Did you visit him alone?"

"Yes. I told you Kahvi was frightened. Why does it matter?" The man paid no attention to this question.

"No one else was in or near the jail—no one but Rembert?"

"I don't know. I don't even know if Rembert was there, unless that's the oxy-waster we've been talking about. Something knocked me out—"

"That was Rembert. He said he thought you were associating with Invaders when he saw—"

"What's an Invader? And what did your friend Rembert do afterward?"

"He came to us." It was the woman again, still paying no attention to Fyn's questions. "Was anyone with you when you regained your senses?"

Earrin hesitated. He was quite incapable of lying, like any Nomad, but he did not want to admit the presence of Bones. Perhaps, since Hillers did not regard the natives as people, the word "anyone" would not include the Observer; but that would still be deceit—misleading communication. It was this, not the mere word "lying," which triggered Fyn's righteousness reflexes.

The hesitation lasted too long.

"Was your wife with you when you awakened."

"No."

"Was anyone—human or not—there." That wording left no choice, nor any ground for hesitation.

"Yes."

"Rembert was right," snapped the woman to the others. "There's one of them following this Nomad. We don't need to know where it is now— even if it's in the jail it won't matter. Bring this Nomad to the Hill."

"But my—" Earrin made a gesture, nearly invisible in the deepening darkness, toward the raft.

"Your wife can do without you for a while. We'll bring her the payment that was promised. You are coming with us. We need bait!"

V

Captive, Curiously

Bones swam rapidly, entirely below the surface. There was no obvious reason to stay near the raft, and there was a burning need to fill the knowledge vacuum about the region beyond the ridge. The way to get there without being seen by the Hillers was obvious enough—swim around the Canton peninsula part way, to its northern extremity, or even all the way around to the western side, under water where human beings couldn't see very well even by daylight. It was almost night now, and even if there were people elsewhere on the shore it should be possible to leave the water without being seen.

There was no problem in finding the way. The Fyn group, with Bones, had been here several times in the last few years, and the Observer knew the terrain—even under water—well enough.

The water was growing darker; the sun had set by now. The almost permanent haze of Earth's new atmosphere still held a golden-brown luminosity, but that would not last long. The distance to swim was scarcely a kilometer, inside the Sayre islets, west across the end of the peninsula for a few hundred meters, then into the cove on the northwest corner. Bones swam steadily.

The water at the head of the little bay finally began to grow shallow, and Bones turned cautiously to get one eye above the surface, folding the broad fin on that side closely against the rubbery body to keep it hidden.

The shore showed no sign of human beings. However, the plants were large—almost treelike—and included many useful varieties of both natural and pseudolife. There were several masses of Newell tissue, the porous material from which the Fyns had made their raft. There were spinneys of realwood, a tough nitro-growth useful in construction; there were tangled masses of the Yamatiya cordage organism. It was the sort of place where human beings might easily be present even at night, sleeping between days of collecting or craft work, and Bones submerged again and went on to the west side, a matter of another three or four hundred meters.

Here, too, the shore was almost a jungle, but the

growths were less useful; slimy patches of various kinds of nitro-life, tangled and thorny bushes and copses of more evolved stuff. It was not certain that there would be no people, but the population of the species was limited. They couldn't be everywhere.

Bones moved inshore to half-meter depth—the water was almost mirror-smooth on this side of the peninsula. It was not practical here to turn one-eye-up without exposing more body anyway, so the Observer's fishlike form rose far enough to use both. The huge eyes made a quick inspection in both directions along the shore, and without attempting to stand upright Bones slipped rapidly across the few meters of open sand and into the concealment of the vegetation. No sound at all resembling a human voice responded to the act, though the Observer could not have been really sure of any such resemblance.

Several minutes of waiting made it reasonably sure that no people had seen. Slowly, carefully, and as silently as the great body could manage, Bones worked inland through the sometimes slippery and sometimes spiky plants. The way led uphill toward the top of the same ridge which had concealed the fire earlier in the day, but for a long time no signs of burning could be found. The Observer worked back and forth—north and south—rather than straight eastward and upward, but for a long time had no luck. This was strange; it was hard to believe that the blaze had not covered a large area. It was almost completely

dark by now, with neither the moon nor the comet
in the sky, but Bones' huge eyes were far more
efficient than those of any human being.

There were no informative sounds, either. The
whips, leaves, branches and spines of the various
plants and plantlike pseudos were moving in the
light breeze to create a background murmur, but
there were no large animals other than human
beings and Observers now on Earth. Bones could
be reasonably sure that none of these was moving
anywhere close by. Perhaps the fire had been of
natural origin after all—still, those people whose
appearance had caused Bones to leave Earrin
alone had been coming from somewhere on this
side of the peninsula. Care was still in order;
would *all* of any group have gone over to the jail?
Maybe, but maybe wasn't safe enough.

Then the risk dropped from consideration as a
faint suggestion of radiant heat manifested itself.
Bones turned slowly until both lateral fins re-
ceived the sensation equally, and for several seconds both great eyes bored without result in the
indicated direction, northward. Then, carefully,
the Observer moved the same way. At first the
surrounding plants interfered with clear vision,
but then the higher growth began to thin out
ahead. After two hundred meters or so there was
even a horizon; stars could be seen nearly down to
the ridge at the right, and almost as low directly
ahead. In the latter direction the points of light
were trembling and quivering more than usual. A
heat source must lie that way.

Fifty meters further along, eyesight confirmed the deduction. Ahead lay a long pile of stones across the researcher's line of travel, a roughly-made wall half the height of a man. For the last ten meters before reaching it there was no vegetation at all, and the ground felt very warm. The wall, or what had been a wall, surrounded a space some fifteen meters across; inside this area lay a bed of still glowing coals.

The whole thing had to be man-made, but what did people want with such a huge fire? What could they learn from it? Or, since it was now pretty clear that human beings had other drives than the hunger for knowledge, what appetite could it satisfy? Certainly not the urge for nourishment which drove the Fyns so relentlessly. What would Earrin, or Kahvi, or Danna get from such an operation? Bones was as willing to speculate as any human being, but much less willing than most of that species to be satisfied with the results of speculation. The hunger for knowledge which characterized the Observer species could no more be satisfied with "maybes" and daydreams than a starving human being could be contented by chewing on a twig. More observed facts would have to accumulate. Bones happily set about finding them.

The stone was typical human tumbled-rock work, except for the lack of any mortar or cement. That might be due to the heat—but hold back on inferences! The rocks themselves were typical of the area, and showed no signs of artifical shaping.

Bones was a couple of thousand years too late to
have seen a New England stone wall—the wild
erosion which had accompanied the atmosphere
change had removed all such loose structures—
and could not read any archaeological implications into the fragments. The Observer was now
sure that the units had reached Earth much
sooner after its atmosphere change than they had
ever managed before. Certainly it was the first
time they had found large, active animal life
which seemed to have survived from the free-
oxygen era; but ideas about possible connections
between that life and the change itself were still
very hypothetical, and a science of archaeology
was still to develop.

The stones were still unpleasantly hot, but
Bones used touch as well as sight to gather data.
There was dried, crumbling dirt on and between
some of the boulders, but no obvious way to tell
whether this had been intended to fill spaces, or
simply too much of a nuisance to clean off when
the rocks had been moved originally. Bones was
inclined to suspect the latter, partly because the
dirt did not occur everywhere and partly because
of the prejudice against unnecessary labor which
Earrin and Kahvi showed so strongly. The pre-
sumption that this was a standard human characteristic was risky but not unreasonable.

Whatever the structure and fire had been intended for, the purpose seemed to have been ful-
filled; there were no people around now. The
fire itself had completed its violent stage only
recently—this would have been obvious even if

Bones had not been watching at the time. Coals from a fire did not last very long with no oxygen to diffuse into the bed, and the Observer had seen plenty of fires since coming to Earth. People who wanted something from the blaze would presumably have waited around to get it, rather than travelling away and back again—this, again, was an inference from the Fyn family behavior, but seemed reasonable.

Having reached this tentative opinion, Bones relaxed some of the precautions to avoid observation and moved more freely around the edges of the big fireplace. This proved to be a mistake, like the inference itself.

Human voices, Bones could not tell how many, suddenly sounded from the west, toward the shore where the researcher had landed. They were not nearly as far away as the shore, but not so close as to remove all hope that the Observer had escaped their sight. The fish-body dropped to horizontal and moved as quickly as all six tentacles—the four normally used for walking and the two handling ones—could carry a hundred and twenty kilograms along the remains of the wall. This speed was normally faster than a human being could run for more than a few seconds, slender as the tentacles were. The internal engineering and biochemistry of the body were very different from those of Earth's former oxygen-using endoskeletal organisms. This time, however, the speed was not great enough.

Bones rose briefly to see how close the people were, and a chorus of yells rose suddenly—clearly

a view-halloa, even though the words were not
distinguishable. Bones dropped back to all sixes,
but the crashing of bushes showed that the human
beings had also put on speed. The Observer was no
longer visible against the sky, which had
brightened in the east with the approach of moonrise, but the people had seen enough.

Bones, originally between them and the fireplace, got around a corner of the latter and headed
toward the east at top speed. Breaking realwood
indicated that the pursuers were spreading out on
each side to forestall any dodging; it looked for a
moment as though Bones would be able to keep
ahead of them over the hilltop and down to the
water on the raft side, which would be enough.
Certainly they could not pursue through water—
human beings simply weren't built for fast
swimming.

However, Bones didn't even reach the top of the
ridge. Fifty meters or more short of that goal, the
ground suddenly became impassable. Wherever a
tentacle touched it, unbearable pain caused the
limb to draw back out of control. The Observer
could not see what was responsible, but in a matter of seconds found it impossible to travel in any
direction. The mysterious agent that caused the
agony had transferred itself to the tentacles. No
matter what they touched now, the pain resulted.

Bones stopped, perforce, and explored the surrounding ground as well as he could with the
tortured limbs. Some places seemed safe, others
produced more of the pain. The Observer brought
one of the injured tentacle tips within reach of the

fine handling tendrils which surrounded the huge mouth, and examined it gingerly. The trouble was clear enough; the tough skin was studded with fine splinters of, apparently, glass. The tendrils could remove these easily enough from the upper and middle tentacles, but the lowest, shortest walking tentacles could not reach or be reached by these delicate appendages. Travel was impossibly painful, and Bones was still doing everything practical to extract the devilish things when the people arrived.

There were five of them, and they swarmed around the Observer closely enough to offer the hope that they might become involved with the glass themselves; but that hope died almost at once. Even in the starlight it could be seen that they were wearing something on their feet. Kahvi, Earrin, and their child had never done this, but their regular outdoor equipment had made the concept of protective garments clear enough to their nonhuman companion.

Bones could make out a few of the words of the chattering group, but without supplemental gestures could get little or no connected meaning. Most city dwellers in Observer memory had shown their hostility by words or, at most, thrown rocks. There was no memory of capture—at least, none which had been passed on. That thought was rather grim, though the closest any Observer unit could come to the fear of death was worry about inability to pass on new information. It had been many months since Bones had transferred memories with another Observer unit. This had been a matter of mild discomfort rather than acute anxiety, since there were so far only a few units on the planet. As long as there was freedom of action, and especially of travel, it could be assumed that a meeting would eventually occur.

Now both these freedoms were threatened, and Bones began to feel a little like a man trapped in a forest fire. The control of the situation was in other tentacles.

Transporting their captive was quite a problem for the human beings. Bones saw no reason to expend energy keeping rigid, and nearly three meters of very limp fish, weighing well over a hundred kilograms, are awkward to handle. They managed it, however, without using the tentacles as drag lines—it did not occur to Bones until much later that they might have done this, or to wonder why they didn't. Two of them shouldered the rubbery mass, one on each side, just behind the eyes, and two more a short way back. The fifth supported the tail flukes. The group started back toward the fireplace, and for a moment Bones wondered if they planned a cremation. Then they turned south toward the big hill, and the tension eased.

For fully an hour they travelled, sometimes uphill and sometimes down, sometimes straight toward Big Blue and sometimes to the right or left of this heading—sometimes, indeed, almost away from it. Bones was not quite sure how much route detail was worth remembering, but played it safe; it might be necessary to retrace the journey or to tell Kahvi or Earrin how to do so.

Finally they reached a small stream winding from the hills toward the eastern bay. A stone building similar to the jail was now visible by moonlight. The water from the stream had been used to improvise an air lock. This was decidedly smaller than the one at the jail, and the carriers had trouble working Bones' limp form through it; but eventually everyone was inside. The people unmasked, opened their oxygen cartridges, and hung them on the walls to equilibrate.

Bones wondered whether these were normal people or oxygen addicts as described by the Fyns, but had no way to tell. From the floor it was not possible to see what sort of plants were on the air trays. The human beings talked desultorily for a while, but finally appeared to sleep. They had not tied their captive in any way, probably believing that the glass splinters were an adequate immobilizing agent. They were quite correct. Otherwise, escape would have been easy. The roof was even lower than that of the jail, and Bones' head would have gone through if the long body had been able to stand up. If these Hillers were anything like the Nomads Bones knew, most or all of them would have stayed to repair the roof rather than pursue.

However, even moving tentacles was painful now. The glass seemed to be working its way deeper as time went on.

It was not quite daylight when the trip was resumed, and there was never a chance to check the building's oxygen sources. There must have been spare cartridges; even a pure oxygen atmosphere would not have recharged the others so soon. As before, the people took for granted that their captive could not walk.

The sky quickly brightened, and Bones was surprised to discover how short a distance they had covered the night before. They were still less than a kilometer from the spot where the raft was anchored; it could be seen from the first hillock they climbed. The stream which had furnished the air lock for the little shelter emptied into the bay only five or six hundred meters south of the jail. Travelling in the dark with an awkward burden must have been far slower than the Observer had guessed.

Not even Bones' eyesight could spot anyone on the raft, but fully a dozen people were busy around the pile of cargo. What they were doing could not be made out before the area disappeared behind the hill. Bones resumed memorizing their travel route.

They were not headed toward any of the Great Blue Hill entrances which Bones knew about. At the moment, the goal seemed to be the nearer and lower eminence called Hemenway. Neither Kahvi nor Earrin had ever mentioned that the city extended that far, but this of course was no proof that it didn't. Also, of course, there was no proof that the captive was being taken to the city.

Travel was faster than in the dark, but not much straighter, and the sun had climbed well above the horizon when they came to a large pool on the eastern slope of Hemenway, in the notch between that eminence and Hancock. Bones did know the place names; the elevations were visible from the bay, and Nomads used place names wherever possible. They were sticklers for unambiguous communication, and a name was far more definite—and quicker to get across—than "the second-highest you can see to the east of Big Blue—you know, the one with the darker vegetation and the cloud over it." Even with Bones' hearing deficiencies it was usually possible to recognize a slowly-uttered, isolated, polysyllabic word.

The pool was clearly artificial and was presumably an air lock, though it was large enough to be used by dozens of people at once. There was no trouble getting Bones through it this time, since the Observer's tissue was a good deal denser than water and did not resist being pulled below the surface.

All question about what might happen, all worry about the Fyns, everything extraneous vanished from Bones' mind and attention. As far as memory went, no Observer had ever been inside one of the human cities. Even the ominous implication of this fact shrank to insignificance; here was a chance to learn, to observe, to remember. The problem of passing the knowledge on could be faced later.

At first there was little to see. The air lock opened into a cave about fifty meters wide and long, and five or six high—the roof was far from even. The light was dim but adequate, radiating from large, irregular patches on ceiling and walls. What made them luminous was something else to be learned; from what Bones knew of human technology, pseudolife was again the best guess. At the moment there was no way to check as the captive was carried rapidly across the cave to the mouth of a tunnel wide enough to take both the party and equally large groups going the other way. There were dozens of people around, but most of them seemed to avoid the Observer and the young captors. A few joined the group; all these seemed young, too, and there was much conversation which Bones could not, as usual, follow.

Half a dozen times the party turned into other passages, sometimes one way and sometimes the other. The turns were seldom exact right angles, and Bones' sense of direction, which like that of the average human being depended entirely on memory if there were no sun or other long-range reference body, began to grow very shaky.

There were numerous doorways along the passages, some open and others blocked by doors. Bones was still trying to set up a reliable memory scheme for keeping count of these when the party turned into one of them.

The room they entered might have been called either a workshop or a laboratory. There were masses of wood, Newell tissue, and other structural materials lying around. Table tops bore tools of glass, stone, and even copper, as well as partly finished artifacts of obscure nature. There was another door on the far side.

They went through this. The next room was nearly bare, measuring some ten meters each way. The far quarter was separated from the rest by a set of bars extending from ceiling to floor. It was too dark to see just what the bars were made of and in any case Bones would not have noticed. They made a very weak call for attention compared to the other Observer beyond them.

VI

Invaders, Indefinitely

Kahvi saw the people talking to her husband, but paid little attention. They had been expecting someone to come for the cargo, of course. The woman herself was busy with the routine of the raft—trimming and feeding oxygen and nitrogen plants, removing fruit and meat from other growths, feeding Danna and herself, making sure the child understood everything that was being done and letting her do much of it herself—educating her daughter; establishing the multitudinous hangups necessary for survival outside the cities. Some day the girl would have to do all this without help or supervision; her parents were already in their middle twenties.

The tent tissue had to be examined, as did the material making up the floats. Both were pseudolife products which sometimes continued to "live" in unexpected and inconvenient ways. There was much less leisure for a Nomad than for a city-dweller.

Danna, a normally intelligent five-year-old, was always asking questions. This evening she produced one which took her mother's attention entirely away from the shore for some time. The child already knew much about pseudolife—the self-replicating chemical growths developed long before the chance in Earth's atmosphere to carry out various tasks or produce desired substances without human attention. She had seen many varieties, not only the Newell "plants" which produced structural material for the raft, and the photosynthetic producers of breathing oxygen, but even the metal-reducers which "lived" in the ocean and brought in copper, chromium, uranium, and other elements. She had grasped the general idea that pseudolife was human-designed and, originally, human-made and therefore "artificial" as opposed to "natural."

She had, however, recently become aware of the expected sibling—she had been too young to be really aware of the others which had survived birth by only a few days or weeks—and become more realistically aware of her own origin. Now, naturally, she wanted to know why she herself was not artificial if her parents had "made" her.

Kahvi had no more luck with the ensuing discussion than parents had ever had before her, but it took all her attention for well over an hour. Danna had finally gone to sleep, dissatisfied and somewhat cranky, and the mother could once more turn her attention to the outside world and realize that Earrin had not yet come back.

She did not worry at first. Her husband might have had to do almost anything once the customers arrived—perhaps help carry the cargo to some other place, or go to fetch the payment. However, after some minutes of thought and several more of straining her eyes uselessly into the darkness, Kahvi checked the cartridge status by touch, assembled and donned her outdoor equipment, and slipped silently into the water. There was nothing to be afraid of in the sea except its trace of nitric acid, and she was as used to that as her ancestors had been to the far more deadly automobile. There were no surviving real-life animal forms other than humanity from before the change; and in spite of the nitro-life's tendency to easy mutation and consequent rapid evolution it had produced no animals much above microscopic size. None of these had developed the ability to parasitize human beings, though some were dangerous to air-cultures and other human necessities.

Kahvi surfaced at the land end of the raft with all her attention, therefore, directed toward the shore. Nothing could be seen or heard but the ripple of waves on the beach, even with the tent tissue no longer in the way. She listened and looked for several minutes, and finally waded ashore. Dimly aided by vision, she found where they had stacked the cargo. It was still there. Finally she called out her husband's name. "Earrin? Where are you?"

The answer was not in Fyn's voice, and she started violently. "He's not here, Kahvi Mikkonen, but is in no trouble."

"Where is he? Why didn't he tell me he was going? Who are you?"

"There was some danger, and we took him up to the hill."

"What danger? The fire? We thought that was out, and—"

"Not the fire. It *is* out." The voice, originally some tens of meters away, was coming closer, though Kahvi could not yet see its owner. "I don't want to frighten you, but your husband was being followed by an Invader."

"What's an Invader? And who are you? I don't recognize your voice, but—"

"But you've seen me before. I'm Jem Endrew. I met both of you when you were delivering copper a long time ago. Surely you've seen Invaders; you Nomads must meet them far oftener than those of us who live underground. They look like—well, maybe you've never seen a book with a picture of a fish." There was just a suggestion that the voice had been going to continue, and Kahvi suspected that the Hiller had just stopped himself from adding, "Maybe you've never seen a book."

"I have," she replied. "They look a little like the metal-feeders we get your copper from."

"I've never seen even a picture of those," Endrew admitted. "Anyway, the Invaders have long bodies, anywhere from half or three quarters of a meter to two and a half or three. They're fish-shaped, as I said. A big one is maybe a third of a meter wide at the widest part, and not quite as thick. The tail goes sideways instead of up and down, and there are two long sort of flaps or fringes along the sides. They swim with a sort of up-and-down bending of the body and flaps and tail. There's a big eye on each side in front of the flap, and a long ropy arm between the eye and the flap. The mouth goes across the top of the head—or the front, if it's swimming—and opens sideways, and has little ropy arms around it. There are more of the ropy things in back—I'm not sure just how many. You'd think they were too thin, but the Invader can stand up on them and even run faster than a man. You really haven't seen one?"

Kahvi was tempted to evade, but Nomad hang-ups overrode the urge.

"Oh, I've seen them, of course. We don't call them—what was it—Invaders. Are they common here? Didn't you used to call them Animals? I've only had a really good look at one of them." The last statement was a strain; it was the truth, in a way, but certainly a truth likely to deceive.

"They're not really common," replied Endrew. "Yes, they used to be called Animals until we learned better. What do *you* call them?"

Again the habit of truthfulness prevailed. "Natives."

"What? But that's ridiculous! A native is a—a

person who is born in a place, and whose parents and grandparents have been—it's someone who *belongs.* How can one of these things *belong*? *We're* the natives!"

"How can we be?" Kahvi asked in astonishment. "We can't even live here without special equipment. We have to breathe oxygen, and we have to have real or pseudo plants to make that by photosynthesis. There aren't enough of those to make a whole world full of oxygen, and if there were there are too many other plants to take the oxygen and make nitric acid. You've been taking your mythology too seriously. Calling people natives is simply silly. I suppose we must be natives of somewhere, but it certainly isn't this world."

"That's right—you probably went to a Surplus school, didn't you?" sneered the Hiller. "They never told you about the change—that Earth used to have air people could breathe. It was the Invaders who made the change, and destroyed the oxygen."

"They taught me the change myths, all right," retorted Kahvi, "but they claimed it was human beings who made the change with science. I don't see why I should believe any of the stuff they taught in Surplus school—all they really wanted was to convince me it was right and proper for me to be aborted from Blue Hill on my twelfth birthday."

"From Blue Hill? You're one of our Nomads?"

"I was born in Blue Hill, the third child of my highly respectable parents, and therefore Surplus. You're a bit young to remember—and of course you wouldn't have been in contact with such undesirables anyway."

She stopped, realizing that her temper had made her say too much. Neither she nor her husband cared greatly about their state of exile—both liked the Nomad life; but they had decided long before that if their "home" cities happened to forget them, trading and other relationships would be more comfortable. Most city-dwellers were more negative about their "own" Nomads than others, for reasons not obvious to either of the Fyn family adults. Presumably Endrew would be the same.

If he was, though, it didn't show. There was no change in his tone as he answered, "Thanks for telling me. That must have happened, as you say, before I was old enough to know. Abortions don't happen very often, after all; the last one was when I was about eight, and that was an older person. I might tell you about that some time, if you don't mind listening to something besides mythology—and don't mind risking the discovery that what you think is mythology really happened."

"One Surplus school is enough, thanks." Kahvi was just barely polite. "I must thank you also for telling me about my husband, and trying to protect him from your—Invader, if that's what you call the natives. I'm sorry you had to wait so long; you could have come to the raft to tell me."

"Your husband had already started with the others when I was told to wait to tell you. He said nothing about sharing your air. I had the jail nearby for recharging if I needed to."

"Thanks again. I hadn't realized he went un-willingly."

"How do—what makes you think he did?"

"Something you just told me. I'll keep the de-tails. I'm not worried about what the 'Invaders' might do to Earrin, but I hope he's safe with your friends. If you don't need our air, I'll go back to get some sleep. I will come ashore in the morning to complete whatever arrangements are in order about the cargo—and about my husband. Breathe freely."

"Breathe freely." The dark figure made no at-tempt to dispute her implied charges, and moved away toward the jail with no further words.

Back on the raft Kahvi could not sleep, though she couldn't guess why. She was not really wor-ried about Earrin, in spite of her words to En-drew; she could not really believe that Hillers, or any other city-dwellers, who Nomadded their Surplus children so they could ignore the un-pleasant fact of what usually happened to them, would actually resort to violence. What they wanted him for was still unclear, but she expected to see him again unharmed.

Danna was where she belonged, breathing quietly. The life support plants all smelled as they should—Kahvi got up and checked them again, after a while, as the most likely source of her wakefulness. Bones' absence was a little unusual, but not really surprising. Kahvi knew enough about her drives to guess that there would be information the next day about what had gone on at the fire site. The fire itself must have been caused by Hillers, since there had been no lightning in the Boston area for days.

What did these people want with all that metal and glass? She and Earrin had wondered after receiving the order, but had found no answer which they could believe. There was little use now for either material. Glass furnished smooth surfaces for growing tissue sheets, and of course sharp edges. Copper was mostly used for art work, though it was sometimes hammered into tools which needed no edge, or at least no durable one.

Earrin had never been inside the Blue Hill city, and the northern one from which he had been aborted had not given him enough knowledge to make good guesses; its Surplus school had been no better than, if as good as, Blue Hill's. Kahvi knew more about city life, and was better read, than her husband because she had not been Nomadded so young. Most Surplus children, of course, were not ejected; death rates were such that most of them reentered their societies long before reaching the key age of twelve. Kahvi had made it by only one day, and never really recovered from the tension of the preceding few months. She had hated the school, hated the community, hated her status, and for the most part hated her fellow citizens. The school had, of course tried to make her regard the whole system as natural, inevitable, and right. A city had air for just so many people; if any couple had more than two children, the surplus ones could not be kept unless death made room for them. The guilty parents could not, of course, be dispensed with;

they were already useful citizens and real people.
The Surplus children could not, of course, be
destroyed—that would be violence. They were
educated to provide for themselves outside the
city, and aborted at the age of twelve unless re-
prieved by a convenient death. The fact that most
of them died within a few days was never faced.
The failure to credit deaths to children not yet
born was based on historical argument; at first,
when this had been done, a black market in death
records had been developed which had actually
increased the city's population and endangered
the air supply—there was just so much sunlight
per year available to the indoor plants, and there
was seldom any success in growing photosynthetic organisms outside and transporting the oxygen indoors. The net result was that in about two
thousand years the Blue Hill population had
shrunk to about a quarter of its original twelve
thousand.

Kahvi's bitterness had not decreased. She had
had friends both younger and older who had been
Nomadded both during her time in the school and
after she had become a citizen. She had never
been able to forget them. After her reprieve she
had often gone outside with the hope of meeting
one of them among the Nomads who occasionally
passed; she had neither seen nor heard of them.
Shortly after her sixteenth birthday, however, she
had come across human remains in one of the
"jails" scattered around the area to give recently
aborted youths a chance for life and serve as living
quarters for citizens doing necessary work out-

doors. The fragments had not been recognizable as any particular individual, but she had never really gotten over the shock. Also, she had not been at all tactful in her remarks about the system for the next few months, and by the time she was seventeen had won the distinction of being the first adult in over five decades to be Nomadded. She had lived for several months in various jails, improving her survival skills, and then met Earrin with his raft.

The man had been aborted at the normal age from Beehive on the Maine coast, a hundred and fifty kilometers or so north of the Boston area. He had been picked up at once by a long-established Nomad who had taught him the raft life. The older man had already been in his thirties, and had died when Earrin was about fifteen.

Kahvi had taken to the raft to get farther from Blue Hill and its people. Affection for and from Earrin had come later. Their occasional return to the Boston area had always aroused memories, but she had learned to keep them far enough from her active thoughts so that they didn't bother her—much.

Her upbringing had of course made her self-conscious at first about her pregnancies, even though only Danna had survived. Now, however, self-confidence and self-respect had overcome this feeling, and she was now close to the point where she might have bragged about her family to one of her former fellow citizens. This time, common sense had submerged that urge; if the Hillers found out about Danna, some of them at least would feel it their duty to take the child for Surplus education—as a favor to the little one, of course.

Kahvi's mind wandered back toward the present. Invaders? Dangerous? Following Earrin? Obviously some Hiller had seen Bones, very probably the oxygen junkie in the jail had fled to the fire site; the people who had met Earrin could have come from there. Bones, however, had certainly never done anything to worry the citizens of Blue Hill. Were there other natives around? If so, what could they have done? Kahvi couldn't believe that one of them would actually harm a person—at least, she didn't want to believe it; she had left Danna in Bones' care too often in the last five years. Natives ate plants, since there was nothing else for them to eat. They didn't breathe, but as long as they got an appropriate mixture of nitrates and reducers they were all right. Their main drive was curiosity, if Bones were typical. Maybe one of them, or more than one, had tried to get into the city to satisfy that urge; but why should that bother the Hillers? The creatures didn't breathe, so none of their precious air would be lost.

And what had started this crazy notion that the natives had changed the world from a place where people could live outdoors to what it was now? Kahvi had heard various versions of the legend that Earth had once been habitable for people, but had never really believed any of them even in school. There were lots of books, of course, which told of people being outdoors without any mention of breathing equipment, but some things were simply taken for granted, and of course the art of story telling must be nearly as old as humanity itself. Some things were too hard to believe, however entertaining they might be to hear or read.

However, it was a fact that these Hillers seemed to regard natives as genuinely dangerous. This would have to be told to Bones when she came back; it seemed more serious than the mere unpopularity the native had experienced before. Was this what had been keeping Kahvi awake? Bones was a good and trusted friend; the idea of her being treated violently by anyone, and especially by Blue Hill citizens, was more than unpleasant.

Danna stirred in her nest on the other side of the entry hatch, breathed more loudly for a few seconds, and was still again. The unborn child twitched slightly, and quieted. Kahvi remembered nothing more for several hours.

Then the moon was shining on her, a waning gibbous disc high in the south. The comet was following it faithfully, four hours behind. Dawn could not be far away. Kahvi sat up and looked around.

Sea and shore were brighter than by starlight, but still far from clear. There was no wind at all, and only a gentle smell moved the rafts and caused the reflections of moon and comet to undulate. Ashore, everything was still—

No. There was motion. There were human figures by the pile of cargo, and some of the material had certainly been moved. What was going on? Could the Hillers be taking the material in the hope of not paying? That was hard to believe, but at least one of them was an oxygen waster, and that was equally incredible.

Or was one of the figures Earrin? She could not be sure, even unmasked, that all the figures were human, though of course none was as tall as Bones. No, they were people—ordinary people, that is. But what were they doing? Making something from the cargo? Now they had stopped and seemed to be discussing something—they were all together in a group instead of spread over meters of beach.

Now they were all moving away, toward the jail. There were five of them, and they moved slowly, as though they were tired. Kahvi watched as they approached the building and, one by one, disappeared into the air lock, leaving the landscape motionless again except for the reflections on the water.

Kahvi did not have Bones' insatiable thirst for information, but she was a human being with normal human curiosity. Human beings, not being parthenogenic, do have other appetites, but curiosity is still a normal and healthy human emotion, especially in an environment where accurate understanding of what is going on usually means life against death. The hunger for knowledge and understanding, therefore, characterizes intelligent beings of any species until age and waning vitality bring the conviction that everything important is already known. Kahvi, at twenty-five, was elderly, but she had lost very little of her vitality. The Hillers might be sleeping—but they might be talking, especially in a straight-oxygen environment.

Carefully, to avoid waking Danna, the woman donned outdoor gear and slid into the water. Guided by the moon, she was able to stay under water until almost ashore. Carefully she raised her head and looked around; there was nothing moving, near the jail or anywhere else. She stood up and waded ashore as quietly as possible, and once out of the water ran quickly to the building. The air lock was toward her, with the moon shining on its surface, and she watched for ripples which would warn of someone entering it from inside.

Then she ducked quickly around the northern end and into shadow. She paused briefly to catch her breath. Then she climbed the rough stone of the wall as Earrin had done, carefully raised her head above roof level, and looked through the transparent tissue.

VII

Captured, Conditionally

"Bait." The word was strange to Earrin. His Surplus schooling had included very little about the time before the change, and most of that was admittedly legend. He had never seen a fish or any other nonhuman animal native to Earth, and knew nothing of hunting or fishing or trapping. Even to the Hiller who had used the word it was shorn of nearly all its ancient implications except the central one. He did not try to explain it to Fyn.

"Come along," was all he said. The Nomad followed for a few meters and then paused, looking back toward the raft.

"My wife will have to know where I'm going and for how long. Wait while I tell her; I'll be right back."

The man shook his head. "We can't wait. It wouldn't be safe, and no one knows how long you'll be gone anyway. One of us will stay here and tell your wife where you are if she seems concerned." The fellow gestured, and one of the others turned back. The rest gathered around Earrin as though prepared to use physical force to make him come along. The Nomad was surprised, resentful, and curious, but it seemed wisest to focus on the last of these attitudes. He began walking, and talking.

"I still don't see what you want me for. I don't know what 'bait' means, and I don't know why you're bothered by someone following me."

"The someone is one of the Invaders," one of the young women said patiently. "Maybe you don't know about them and their danger to people—we only learned a few years ago ourselves, and haven't had much chance to pass on the knowledge. We'd like to, but no one from the city could get to another, and there aren't many Nomads to take messages. We need you to bring supplies—no one else has ever been able to get us copper. Maybe when we have a good stock you'd carry news for us to Beehive and Providence and other cities."

"I don't know what 'invader' means, either," Earrin pointed out. "I've never seen anything following me around except a native—in fact, I've never seen anything which *could* follow anyone but people and natives. I've heard that you city folk don't like natives much, but they're certainly not dangerous. What we call 'natives' you've always called 'animals,' as I remember. Is that what you mean now by 'invaders?' "

The woman's reaction to Earrin's word choice was much less emotional than Endrew's would be to Kahvi's an hour or so later. Of course, masks hid most facial expression, but it was still light enough to make out body attitudes. She appeared quite calm as she answered; so did the rest.

"Yes, we used to call them animals. No doubt you learned that name in Surplus school—what was your city?"

"Beehive."

"Ah, yes—down East some distance. Well, there was some excuse for calling the creatures natives, of course, when it was thought they were simply animals. They seemed to do no damage. They hung around eating wild vegetation and watching people without hurting them. It was strange that they spent so much time watching, and we wondered if they did have some intelligence and might really be pests if we tried to grow air or food outside as I've heard some cities do."

"They do," interjected Earrin.

"Well, we don't, so we didn't worry about that." Earrin wondered who "we" might be; all of this group were far too young to represent the general thought of the city. "Then, two or three years ago—"

"More like five," cut in one of the young men.

"Some years ago we discovered that they ate other things, and were dangerous."

"What else did they eat? What else is there for

them to eat?" Fyn asked naturally.

"I—I don't like to say it—but—well, I suppose I'll have to or you won't be convinced. A few years ago one of my friends was outside, and saw one of the things watching a work group she wasn't with. After a while it turned away and went off by itself, to a hollow on the hill where it was hard to see. She'd never seen one act that way, and found a place where she could watch. It was standing up, and seemed to be peeling a very thick layer of skin from its front. It put this on the ground when it was all separated, and presently the skin thickened and narrowed and turned into one of them. It had—it had—"

"All right, it produced a child. What's so deadly about that?" Earrin, who had never seen the phenomenon, was interested but had no sympathy with the city attitude toward everything connected with childbirth. These youngsters seemed to be trying to be independent, but had a long way to go.

"It wasn't that. There's nothing wrong with having children, even when they're surplus—we know that. But after a while this thing picked the baby up and handled it, and held it close—"

"That's still all right. We've—go on."

"Then—then it—it—the creature *ate* the child!"

Earrin had nothing to say. It did not even occur to him that the young woman could be exaggerating, much less actually lying, though he realized that Hiller morals did not quite match those of Nomads. He was silent for several minutes while the darkness deepened and the group walked steadily southward. The woman said nothing either, evidently satisfied with the effect she had produced. Earrin could not decide what to think, much less what to say; his mind kept sheering off the implications. Bones had taken care of Danna many times while her parents were out of sight. Finally the man remembered another point.

"You said something about not considering them animals any more. I should have thought this would make them seem more like animals, if what I've heard about animals is true."

"This was something quite different. Actually, only a few of us know about the child-eating—we tried to tell some of the older people and they wouldn't let us get past the first part. They're just stuck in the slime."

Earrin was quite willing to agree with this, but suggested that she come back to the subject.

"All right. I suppose you never learned much about scientific instruments."

"I'm surprised you had a chance to."

"Well, you naturally read books when people tell you not to. A lot of us have—in fact, since you certainly won't tell anyone who matters, all of us and some others have read a lot about—well, such things. Experiments—" one or two of the others murmured disapprovingly at the word—"and things like that." She paid no attention to the sounds. "We work at such things, too, even though some of my less dedicated friends prefer not to use the real words. A few months ago we were setting up something outside, away from the locks and usual work areas where we weren't likely to be found. It was a big sundial; we'd been reading about the way the sun moves in the sky during the year."

"Anyone knows that," remarked Earrin.

"You see it more than we do. Beside, we wanted to—" even the speaker hesitated a little this time—"to measure what was happening." There were no reactions this time from the others. "One of the creatures was watching while we put it together—we'd made the parts in our shop inside. The outside part took several days. On the second day some of the parts had been moved, and a piece I had been going to put in place had been installed by someone else—*not* one of us."

"We checked very carefully the third day, but couldn't be sure anything had been handled. The next day, though, it was really certain. One of us remembered putting a piece in wrong. It was right the next morning."

"How do you know the—the native had done it?"

"Who else could have? It wasn't our group. No one else from the city would have known how. Neither would any Nomad."

"But you didn't *see* it happen."

"Not then." The voice was distinctly triumphant. "We set up another situation—"

"You mean an experiment," Earrin couldn't help remarking.

"Watch it!" growled a male voice.

"Oh no. Just a trial to see that no one from the city could have done it." Darkness and mask saved Earrin from giving away his feelings. These were really children. He hoped Danna could be steered through this stage in a minimum of time. The illogic bothered him; if these youngsters had really rejected the dogma that science had changed the world's air, and were now blaming Bones' people, why did they still feel that scientific words were dirty? The city hangups, evidently, were pretty strong; maybe he should be sorry for the kids.

"How did you do it, and what did you find out?" he asked.

"We started a more complicated dial, got it partly set up, and went inside. A couple of watchers went out through another lock, hid near the work place, and watched—it was still daylight. The Invader waited only a few minutes. Then it went over, put the dial all together, looked at the shadow it made, and then took it apart and put the pieces back where they had been."

"Pretty conclusive, I have to admit." Earrin was not, of course at all surprised, knowing Bones as well as he did—that was just what any of the natives would have done.

"All right, so you're afraid of them. They're smart, and eat their own children. But they're nitro-life, you know; how could they eat a person?"

"Maybe they couldn't, but anyone who would—" the voice trailed away in a shudder, and Fyn again had nothing to say for a time. At last he changed the subject again.

"I don't see yet what you want me for."

"We'll use you to help catch it," a male voice

boomed out of the darkness. "We need more of them to learn how to get rid of the things."

"More of them? You already have some? And why do you want to get rid of them, even if they have unpleasant ways?"

The first woman took up the conversation again.

"Yes, we caught the other one. The night after the test, we sent out a large group from the other lock and surrounded it. It didn't try to get away when we drove it inside. We thought the oxygen would bother it, but it didn't seem to notice any difference. The trouble is that with only one we can't make tests likely to kill it, because then we couldn't learn any more. When we catch this other one we won't have to be so careful."

"You'd be willing to *kill* one? Just because you—"

"It's not because they disgust us. There's a much more important reason. We have a plan, and we can do it if the Invaders aren't here to stop us."

"I suppose you want to change the world's air back." The woman seemed a little startled, and became defensive.

"Why not? And how did you know?"

"I'm a Nomad. I've been through Surplus school. Most of us get that idea while we're learning how to make air for ourselves."

"Well, why not?"

"Because you can't. The more photosynthetic oxygen makers you have working, and the more oxygen they make, the more and faster the nitrate-makers will work. You never get ahead on the oxygen, except in spaces so small that you can control which growths are around. The idea that there used to be an all-oxygen atmosphere is a pleasant myth, but if you'd spent all your life trying to keep yourself breathing, you'd know that's all it ever was."

"Wrong." The woman sounded very sure of herself. "That's the trouble with having been afraid of science for hundreds of years; even people like you, who at least know it's useful, don't really know anything about it. You never had a chance to learn. We've been reading, and we *have* learned. I couldn't explain things like equilibrium constants to you, or the way they apply to ecological systems, but we've found out that if you set up a system of oxygen-producers and enough growths that act as parasites on the nitro-makes, that system will *spread* provided it gets a good enough start. That start is the hard part; we'll have to have a lot of help, a lot of people, to spread the growths in a lot of places at once; and we'll have to get rid of the Invaders, because they must have done the same thing the other way to make the world the way they wanted it. They'd spoil what we were doing, so we'll have to get rid of them. That's why we need more specimens—we don't know how to kill them yet."

"You'd really kill them if you caught them?"

"Only one, just now, so as to learn. We don't want to, of course, but until we're rid of them we can't get the world back the way it was, with air you can breathe, and no need to count children as

Surplus and abort them out into the world as we have to do now. Wouldn't you like to breathe air that wasn't so thin it barely kept you alive?"

"No, thanks." Earrin didn't have to think about that answer. If these people were all oxygen-wasters, he wanted no part of their plans. "The air I breathe is the kind people were made for. The stuff your friend was breathing is wasteful, and makes people silly after a while. Not for me; I have to be able to take care of myself—and one or two other people."

"But can't you imagine walking around wherever you want, without having to wear masks and other protection?"

Earrin could not, in fact, imagine anything of the sort. He didn't believe the world had ever had breathable air, and didn't believe it was possible to change it to such a condition; and he was not at all convinced that it would be a good idea to try. He did not have the intensely religious opposition to everything scientific which characterized the typical city-dweller, but he knew that any new line of action could have unforeseen results. He was willing to test a new air plant, but only one tray at a time. Had he been born a few thousand years earlier into an oxygen-rich atmosphere and grown up with the same attitude, he would have been intelligently cautious about large-scale burning of wood or coal.

He mumbled some answer at the woman without remembering later what it was, and continued to think. The others seemed willing to let him do so; perhaps they hoped he had been impressed.

He was, but not the way they hoped. The main point in Fyn's mind at the moment was a straight piece of logic:the Hillers wanted to use him to help capture Bones. They wanted to kill, or try to kill, the native. Therefore, Earrin Fyn should get himself out of the hands of these Hillers, the sooner the better. He did not add a mental Q. E. D. because his reading background was negligible.

How to get away? There were five of them, some walking ahead and some behind. Whether they were following a real path could not be ascertained in the darkness. In any case, the Hillers must know the area far better than Earrin himself did. He had been to one of the Blue Hill locks a few times, but always by the same route.

Simply starting to run one way or the other was senseless. There would be bushes, and thorn branches, and slime, and rocks to run through, slip and trip on, and be slashed, torn and bruised by. The others wouldn't even have to run to get him.

And if he did get away they could still intercept him. He had enough air to last through the night, probably, if he were not too active. He would have to get to an oxygen supply before his cartridges were done. There were of course many jails scattered about Great Blue Hill, but it would be pure luck if he managed to find one in time even after the moon came up; all he could really count on locating were the jail at the landing place, his own raft at the same spot, and the city itself. His captors, who presumably knew the area, could get to any of these places before he could—

If they knew which one he had in mind. Would

they take the raft, where his wife was, for granted? Would they consider the city, or assume that he wouldn't think of it, or wouldn't want to face the troubles he would encounter inside—Nomads were easily recognizable and very unwelcome in civilized communities which kept track of their air. There really was no good and practical reason to justify his going anywhere but home. It was becoming obvious why they weren't bothering to tie him up or hold him tightly, even if they weren't that confident of their powers of persuasion.

He couldn't go back to the raft or jail; they'd get him easily. In the city—well, even if Nomads weren't welcome, there was something which might be worth doing. Earrin was a slow thinker, but a plan began to form.

"Are we going all the way to the Hill tonight," he asked suddenly. "We rowed a long way today, and I'm tired." This was the truth, though not his principal reason for asking the question. His Nomad no-deceit hangup almost made him blurt out the latter as well, but he controlled himself rather unhappily. He felt even worse when one of the men answered with no sign of suspicion.

"No, we'll stop for rest and air soon—about half way. There's a jail just before the slope gets steep."

"Good. Thanks." Earrin lapsed back into thought. There would be cartridges at the jail. No matter what the air status of his captors, they could restock quickly and, probably, beat Fyn back to the raft. Nothing was changed there.

If he merely got out of their sight, that was probably what they would do; and even if they caught him later, one thing might be accomplished. If Bones were actually following, it would be possible to give him a warning about the new and more serious intentions of these Hillers. If, as seemed more likely, he were not, then Fyn could go on to the city and do something about the other native. Bones was the only one of the beings he knew, but he was prepared to regard them all as friends in spite of the woman's horror story; he couldn't attach much weight to the words of these young people even though he couldn't bring himself to believe that they would lie. He knew it was an inconsistent attitude, but every time he tried to resolve it one way or the other his head refused to work. It was easiest to believe that the kids had misunderstood something.

So he would go to the city, which seemed easy enough as long as his present captors could be persuaded to go elsewhere, and maybe something could be done about the other captive. Fyn's general background doomed him to a certain naivety.

It also inclined him to unhesitating action once he had decided what had to be done. There was only one thing to wait for, and that should come before they reached the jail.

It did. They were long out of sight of the bay—unlike Bones' captors a few hours later, this group had gone to the west of the low hills near the base of the Canton peninsula—so moonrise itself could not be seen; but the sky framing the high ground to their left gradually brightened, and at last Earrin felt that he could travel without actual disaster.

"Nearly there?" he asked.

"A couple of hundred meters," came an answer. "You'll see it when we get by that patch of brush."

They did. As might have been foreseen by anyone familiar with jail construction, they were near the bottom of a small gully, and as usual its brook had been applied to the arrangement of an air lock. Details were a little different; the stream seemed to run right under the building, and he wondered for a moment whether this one had two locks. He did not waste time trying to find out.

"Breathe Freely!" he cried suddenly, and at the same moment he broke to his left up the hill. Moonlight showed fairly clear ground, and he made good speed. He had told the truth about being tired, of course, but he was in better physical condition by far than the city people. Two of the men sprang after him, but lost ground rapidly. The woman's voice sounded after them.

"Let him go, idiots! Come in here and recharge. We can get him easily enough!" Fyn didn't bother to look back to see whether the order was obeyed. It was as he had guessed; they would replace their breathing cartridges and go back to the raft area to wait for him. They might even go to the raft itself and wake up Kahvi, but they wouldn't search it. She could say truthfully that he wasn't there. Fyn himself could continue without interference eastward over the hilltop as long as he was in sight of the Hillers, and then on the other side turn south. He had air for most of the night, he knew. Even though he didn't know the area very well, Great Blue Hill could not be missed, and he knew there were several entrances. After finding one he could improvise.

It actually took a good deal longer than he had expected to find an air lock, though he came at the hill from what he believed was the same direction he had always come before. The moon was high, the comet up, and he was starting to feel a little tense about breathing before he finally saw a pool which had to be an entrance to the city. There was no one around it, at least outside, as was to be expected at this hour.

For a few minutes he hesitated. He suddenly realized how little he knew about what might lie ahead. Bones had not appeared—no surprise; Fyn had been sure the Hillers were wrong about his "follower." It would be nice to have the native for company, though. Of course, there was nothing to be afraid of; the worst they would do would be to eject him, and even then they would give him enough air to reach the raft. His former captors would be there, but at least he would be no worse off.

He glanced back at the bay, over two kilometers away, and wondered whether he could actually see the dark spot of the raft on the brightening water. He wondered why he sometimes did things without thinking them through, decided it was because there was so seldom sufficient time for that when emergencies arose.

Then he entered the pool.

JANET AULISIO

VIII

Doubt, Duplicated

The other unit was lying on a pad of some material, presumably one of the pseudolife products so freely used by the human beings. It saw Bones at once, and in a single smooth movement came to its full height. This was little more than three quarters that of a typical human being; evidently this unit had been a bud not long before.

It took two or three steps toward the newcomers and was stopped by the bars. Bones tried to wriggle free and cross the rest of the gap, but for some seconds had no luck. The bearers were unable to hold on, and allowed the suddenly not-so-limp form to drop to the stone floor, but they promptly

piled on, seizing every available limb and pre-
venting travel. Bones' emotions did not match
human ones very closely, but the howl of pain
emitted by one of the people who grasped a glass-
studded walking tentacle was rather satisfying
even though the agony was mutual.

Then a brief burst of human words sounded.
"Let it go. See what they do. Keep the doorway
blocked." Bones couldn't tell whether a male or a
female was speaking, partly because of hearing
system deficiencies and partly because the difference still meant nothing whatever to Observers,
but three or four of the monosyllables carried
meaning. It was no surprise when the human beings let go and stood back.

The Observer could not stand; the pain in the
rear walking tentacles was too great. The other
limbs, however, were able to drag the streamlined
form toward the bars and, when these were
reached, to lift it nearly upright.

The smaller figure's upper tentacles lashed
around Bones' body; the larger one reciprocated.
The rubbery forms could not actually squeeze between the bars, but were flexible enough for what
was needed.

On what corresponded to the human chest of
each of the fishlike forms was a disc of specialized
tissue a dozen centimeters across. Its color was
little different from the olive green and brown
mottling of the rest of the bodies; neither Earrin
nor Kahvi had ever noticed it.

Now the two discs pressed together as the tentacles tightened. Neither Observer felt the pain
from the bars also being squeezed between them;

neither felt anything but ecstasy. Neither had communicated for a long time. Memory cells flowed from one body to the other through the discs for more than a minute before the embrace relaxed, and for many more seconds the two held motionless while the transferred memories spread through their bodies, duplicated and re-duplicated, and gradually as the glow faded rose to conscious level.

When they finally separated, each was as nearly identical to the other in mind and memory as living creatures can ever be. Bones *remembered* everything that had led up to the smaller unit's capture, and what had happened to it since then. The other *remembered* Bones' experience with the Nomads for the last several years; it knew Earrin and Kahvi and their child; it would, on meeting any of them, be able to use the sign language which they and Bones had worked out to supplement oral speech, and it would understand human words as well as Bones, with the same auditory limitations, could.

It knew Bones' pain, and immediately on emerging from the pleasant daze which accompanied memory transfer the smaller being dropped to the floor and began removing with its fine-handling mouth tendrils the glass splinters which Bones had been unable to reach.

The Observer wondered how the human beings would react to this, and rolled an eye or two in their direction. Surprisingly, only two people were now visible. Both were in the doorway, and both had their back turned to the Observers. The latter could not even guess at the reason for this behavior; the memory that Kahvi and Earrin preferred to be alone when they communicated bore no obvious relevance.

For several more minutes the smaller being extracted glass, twice pausing for another brief embrace to firm the memory of where the splinters were located. Some of them had gone too deep to be seen or grasped, and had to be squeezed out with the aid of the more powerful handling tentacles.

Eventually Bones was able to stand with reasonable comfort, though healing would take time. What should be done next was too obvious to be a matter for communication, though details were foggy. There was much to be learned about the underground city, since neither unit had seen much of it. This would require getting out of their present location and away from human control. The smaller unit, behind bars, would have the greater trouble with this. The concept of doors and locks for other than environmental purposes, as in a spaceship, was foreign to the Observer mind, but they did remember how the prisoner had gotten into the cage originally. They were completely defeated by the padlock; the finer handling tendrils could get into the keyhole and determine the interior structure fairly well, but were not nearly strong enough to move any useful components. The smaller unit had of course found this out long before. There was a mystery here. Since the keyhole was obviously far too small for any human appendage, and no tool was present to do the job, the whole device must be intended to be opened only by some selected *individuals*. The concept of individual intelligence was growing,

but the idea that some might act in direct conflict
to the interest of others—even the idea that individuals could have conflicting interests—had not
yet taken root in the Observer mind. Bones
thought seriously of going to the door, getting the
attention of a human being, and seeking help with
the lock.

The idea was dismissed after a moment; clearly
the people did not want the Observers free to
travel. However, there seemed nothing more to be
learned here; there was nothing of interest in the
room except pad, bars, and lock, and both units
already knew all about these that their unaided
senses could learn.

Bones therefore walked to the door and pulled
gently on the shoulder of one of the human beings.
The latter turned at once, and almost as quickly
began to speak. The units could not get enough of
the words to make connected sense of them.

"They've finished!" was the cry that caused the
other people to turn their attention back to the
room. "The big one's trying to get out!"

"Don't let it!" another voice called emphati-
cally. "Three of you keep the door blocked. Get
anyone outside to help. The rest, inside. Drive it
into the cage—who has the key?"

"I do."

"All right, you get the lock off and be ready to
open the cage door when we get it near." One of
the human figures slipped past Bones. Three
more—the group had increased in numbers—
spread out to each side of the now blocked doorway and then converged toward the nearer captive. Bones could understand well enough that the
idea was to get the second unit into the cage, and

that this would require the opening of the door.

Two sets of bulging eyes kept the human beings covered. The owners were not in real communication, but none was necessary; their minds had blended so recently that each knew what the other would think and how the other would act—though of course neither thought of the other as an other.

Bones retreated to within two meters of the cage door, and saw it open under the handling of one of the people. As it did so, both Observers acted at once. The smaller one hurtled through the opening, colliding with the woman who had unlocked it and sending her to the floor. Bones' handling tentacles simultaneously grasped two of those approaching and jerked them violently forward. One stumbled as intended and staggered through the door into the cage; the other kept his feet but came between Bones and the other humans. The two Observers raced around the off-balanced group and drove into the ones blocking the doorway. Their momentum was ample to break up the plug.

There were no other people in the work room outside, and the escaping pair raced across it to the only door. Beyond this was the corridor through which they had been brought. Naturally, they separated; there was nothing to be gained by both seeing the same things. The smaller unit headed to the right, the direction which led back to the air lock.

There were people in the tunnel that Bones followed, but not very many. Most of them went to some pains to avoid contact with the Observer. Presumably there would sooner or later be some organized effort to recapture the escaping pair, but there was no way of guessing how long this might take. For one thing, it would have to depend on communication, and this would have to be a slow process with the sound code—though the Observer still had doubts that this was really the only method available to the human species.

Bones had no thought of hiding to avoid capture; this would have defeated the prime objective of learning as much as possible about the city and its inhabitants. This in fact called for communicating with the latter if at all possible, but apparently it wasn't. None of the beings seemed even to realize that the waving appendages indicated a desire, much less an attempt, to talk to them. They either fled rapidly or backed cautiously away, usually producing loud sounds at the same time.

That left little to learn except the pattern of the tunnels and the nature of any artifacts which might be found. The former had already given trouble, since they were not very straight; within minutes the Observer had to give up hope of finding, except by chance, either the lock through which the capture party had come or even the scene of the recent partial escape. Horizontal directions were bad enough, and it was obvious that the city extended vertically as well.

At first it seemed wise not to leave the level of the lock until its details had been learned; there might be a need to leave the city. However, it was hard to see how such a need could arise, or could possibly carry as much weight as the need to learn, and presently Bones was as thoroughly lost in the third dimension as in the first two. It was

not even possible to keep track of levels; the floors
of Blue Hill were anything but horizontal. Boston,
long before, had bragged that its street pattern
represented the paving of the early settlers' cow
paths. The settlers' descendants, who had exca-
vated Blue Hill when it became evident that the
change in Earth's atmosphere could not be
stopped, had similarly been guided by conven-
ience in attacking the local geology. About the
only rule had been to refrain from penetrating an
existing room or tunnel without prior arrangement. There were corridors, living rooms, storage
rooms, workshops, and large and small spaces
whose purposes were beyond the Observer's ability to guess in spite of years with the Fyn family.

The incredible part was that all were deserted.
There had been no human beings in sight since the
first half hour or so after the escape. This would
have been incomprehensible even if Bones had
known about the more than seventy percent population drop since the city had been founded;
surely the people would have been scouring the
tunnels for the escaped aliens. By rights, they
should have been back in custody within an hour
of their escape; neither knew anything of the city,
even the way out. Neither had anything which
would serve as a weapon, and neither would have
thought of using such a thing anyway. A population with any sort of organization and any agreement about what should be done would have had
no trouble either in finding or securing their lost
prisoners.

The fact was, of course, that the group which
had done the capturing was neither representa-

tive of the Hill population in general—as both
Kahvi and Earrin were beginning to realize—nor
particularly well organized. This was a conse-
quence of the limited human communication
faculties which Bones had so far come nowhere
near to foreseeing. Both organization and its re-
verse where concepts which went with a population of individuals.

Bones, therefore, had time to learn much detail
about the city. Unfortunately, none of it led to
meaningful generalizations, even when combined
with the several years close observation of the
Nomad family. It was trivial stuff.

Eventually the researcher began to feel hungry.
This was ordinarily a minor matter; practically
any nitro-life that grew was acceptable food as
long as reasonable balance was maintained between oxidizing and reducing vegetation. Inside
Blue Hill's caverns and corridors, however, there
was no vegetation—the bioluminescent panels
didn't count. Thoughtful consideration of this
problem suggested specific action.

There was oxygen in the city, since the people
went unmasked. Therefore, there were plants—
photosynthetic organisms, synthetic or otherwise, similar to those maintained by Kahvi and
Earrin on their raft and the various places on land
where they sometimes stayed. These plants would
presumably be edible, or have edible parts—
many of the pseudolife forms contained nitrates,
though it was perhaps a bit doubtful that these
would be found inside a human city.

In any case, such plants would need sunlight; no
other energy source could be available to human

beings, judging by the Nomads' attitude toward
fire. Sunlight would be most available in the outer
portions of the hill, and one way to get near the
outside was to go up. As a matter of fact, both
Kahvi and Earrin had occasionally mentioned
that the food and air sources of the cities were
normally on the top levels.

Bones, therefore, began taking every upward-
slanting tunnel that presented itself. This quickly
changed the surroundings, though not for the
reason which might have been expected. Hemenway had not originally had an air plant section;
the whole city was supplied from Great Blue Hill.
The last few years, however, had brought changes.

The tunnels were brighter; there were more of
the luminescent panels on walls and ceiling, and
they appeared to be watered and fed more carefully. If Bones had possessed a sense of smell it
would have been obvious that the air was fresher;
even without it, there was a certain subtle difference in the environment. The area was lived in.

The impression was quickly supported more
objectively. Within the same five minutes, Bones
met two human beings. Both were adult, but con-
siderably younger than Kahvi and her husband.
Both reacted to sight of the Observer by a rapid
retreat, accompanied by high-volume use of their
voices. Both retreated in the same direction;
Bones was, of course, following the first when the
second came on the scene. It seemed likely that
they would lead the way to more interesting
areas, so the Observer matched speeds with them
instead of catching up as would have been so easy.

The chase went on for several minutes without
the cries of the human beings eliciting any re-

sponse. Then an unusually steep upward ramp
showed much brighter light at the top, light
tinged with the golden color of sunlight filtered
through an atmosphere containing distinct traces
of nitrogen dioxide. Bones reached the foot of this
slope just as the second of the people disappeared
at the top, and started up without hesitation.
There was clearly something to see up here.

This proved correct, though the fleeing human
beings had vanished. The sloping tunnel emerged
at one side of a chamber some twenty meters
square, roofed with the same transparent tissue
used on the raft and the jail—Bones did not know
the difference in the latter building. As with the
jail, the tissue was supported at frequent intervals
by thin beams—mere poles—of realwood. The sun
was a brassy patch visible high in the south; only a
few clouds showed in the golden sky.

The room contained at least two dozen tables of
the sort which carried plant trays in the jail, and
most of these did carry flat, bubble-topped boxes
in which growths of various shapes and colors
could be seen. Few of these, however, bore close
resemblance to the oxygen and nitrogen producers Bones knew from raft life. A few had the green
of chlorophyll, but most were of strange reds,
browns, and yellows. They might have been
transplaneted from among the nitro-life forms
which covered most of the world outdoors, though
it was hard to imagine Hillers doing such a thing,
and the shapes of the organisms were mostly un-
familiar.

There were also vats and tanks full of variously
colored liquids. Some of these also held plants;
the others might represent cultures of micro-

scopic real- or pseudo-life. The place might have
been a laboratory, though that was also hard to
imagine of Hillers.

There were doors in all the walls; the light
beyond them indicated that they led to rooms
which also had transparent ceilings. It appeared
that Bones was at the top of the hill. Human voices
sounded loudly, apparently through several of the
doorways. The fleeing human beings had been out
of sight when the Observer reached this level;
there was no way to guess which opening they had
used. It didn't seem to matter much; there was
plenty to keep an Observer occupied for hours in
this room alone.

For one thing, some of the growths were probably edible. This seemed as good a time as any to
find out, since Bones felt an increasing need for
food. Two long tentacles, terminating in four dig-
its the size of a grown man's little finger, lifted
the bubble-shaped transparent top from the
nearest table, placed it carefully on the stone
floor, and began to remove the orange objects, the
size and shape of hen's eggs, from the branches of
the growth within.

Taste, to Bones, was neither "good" nor "bad."
The material had little if any nitrate, but was
adequate for the reducing portion of Observer
diet. The nonhuman consumed all the objects,
replaced the bubble cover on the planter, and
went on to the next. And the next. Why there was
time for so much eating was never clear; the
human voices in the nearby rooms kept up their
chattering. They rose and fell—the idea of *argument* was of course completely foreign to
Bones—but the fourth lid was just being removed

when action finally replaced words. Fully a score of people suddenly poured through the various doors and spread out inside.

They were still chattering—or rather, a few of them were; the others maintained silence and simply looked at the intruder. All carried implements which Bones had never seen before. They were rods, apparently of realwood like the roof poles, about a meter and a half in length, somewhat like the fire sponges. Their ends, however, bore glass blades much thinner at the edges than Earrin's knives, ending in sharp tips, and symmetrical on either side of the axis defined by the wooden handles. Bones had never seen a spear or any other kind of weapon; presumably these things were tools, but their function was completely obscure—

For just a moment. Then one of the human beings uttered a sharp syllable, and eight of the creatures raised the weapons and hurled them at the Observer. It did not occur to the latter to dodge; fortunately the Hillers were almost as unpracticed with the devices as their intended victim. Only one shaft struck its target directly, though the others came close enough to suggest that dodging would probably have been ineffective anyway.

The one point caught the fishlike form a few centimeters below the top of the lateral fins and just in front of the left one. It emerged behind the other at about the same height, proceeded for about half the weapon's length, and left Bones standing transfixed by the spear as effectively as though its wielder had been practicing for years.

It hurt.

IX

Arson, Aggravated

The jail was not very well lighted. There were a few trays containing the luminous pseudolife, but they were scattered among the tables rather than arranged on wall panels as was usual in the cities. In a way this was bad for Kahvi, since lights which covered the inside of the building effectively would have made her less visible. If she had been at all careless, the moonlight would have revealed her easily. She almost made one mistake; the golden bracelet on her left wrist clicked against the stone as she reached the top of the wall. She quickly pushed it farther up toward her elbow until it was too tight to move freely, and carefully kept the arm itself toward the outside of the wall. Moonlight glinting from the metal to an eye inside could hardly help being noticed.

There were six people in the building. She had no way of being sure whether or not any of them was Endrew, though it seemed likely. Who the others might be she could only guess, with no real basis even for that; and since she distrusted guessing almost as much as Bones did, she simply listened. The roof tissue did not block sound effectively, and the excitement of high oxygen made the voices of those below quite loud by Nomad standards anyway. One of them, in fact, was mentioning this very point.

"We can't afford to get too happy," he was saying. "It should take that idiotic Nomad at least half an hour to get back here, cutting around the way he would have to, but at least two of us should be outside to spot him when he does."

"Why?" asked another. "I'm tired, I haven't been able to relax in decent air all night or all yesterday, and I don't see why it's important if he gets back to his raft. If one of those creatures is around, even if it's following him, there must be better ways to catch it. We could make traps with Barefoot's Bane all around, instead of just by the lab."

"The former lab, if you can't remember to call it the Learning Center," remarked another male voice.

"You could have done your objecting earlier!" snapped a woman. "I'm just as tired as you are, and if you really had a better plan to offer—you know there isn't enough Bane either harvested or growing to cover the whole countryside—you could have mentioned it and saved all of us all this outdoor travel."

"I did suggest another and you laughed at it," was the retort. "I pointed out that if an Invader were really following the Nomad around it would mean that its curiosity had focussed on him, and there wouldn't be any way to distract it. I said—"

"That's enough!" the first male voice cut across the rapidly rising tones of the second. "You and Wilma get your gear on, go outside, and start sorting that cargo—get the glass separated and opened where we can use it. We need the new lab as soon as possible. We'll build it right there to save carrying time; we'll get the other material as soon as the sun's high enough tomorrow. You two have had enough straight oxygen for now."

"But—" came the woman's voice.

"But nothing. Both of you. Now. Get dressed!"

Kahvi rather expected more effective resistance to the command, though she had never heard a full-grown argument between authority and subordinate. It was hard for her to believe that city-dwellers could display as much discipline as a normal Nomad, and even harder to credit the notion that oxygen junkies could have any discipline at all. When two of the figures stood up and began to don outdoor equipment she was so surprised that for some seconds she failed to consider how this might affect her own situation. The two were entering the air lock when she suddenly realized how visible she would be the moment they got to the north of the jail.

She thought quickly, weighing necessities. If

she left her present place of vantage she would
hear no more, and information was really vital.
She had, on the other hand, already learned
enough to guide a good deal of action, and being
seen would complicate matters most undesirably.
Further information would have to wait.

She descended the wall quickly and silently,
and lay down in its shadow—standing, she would
show in silhouette against the moonlit ridge. She
heard the people emerge from the air lock pool,
and a moment later saw them pass. Neither
looked in Kahvi's direction. The few words of their
conversation she heard added nothing to her fund
of useful knowledge.

What should she do now? There was no worry
about Earrin for the moment; she had been with
him for over seven years, and was perfectly certain that he was not going to come back to the raft
very soon. She had no idea why he had gone with
the Hillers or why he had left them, but after the
latter move he would certainly have known that
they could intercept him if he came home. She
could not guess what he might be up to, but until
he accomplished it, or decided that he couldn't
accomplish it, her obvious job was to maintain
control of the situation here—keep Danna safe,
and keep the raft available and functioning as a
breathing place.

With these facts worked out clearly, it became
obvious that she had made a tactical error. The
two oxygen junkies were between her and the raft.
The night was clear, the moon high, and the vegetation not nearly heavy enough to conceal a
human figure attempting to cross the beach and

enter the water unseen. Worse, if for any reason they decided to visit the raft itself, she could not possibly get there ahead of them and they would certainly find Danna.

That would be undesirable. Twice during Kahvi's own time in Surplus school she had seen children of Nomads brought in. The Hillers, of course, had been perfectly certain that they were doing the children and their parents a favor, and that the education they supplied would improve life duration and quality for the former; but the captives had felt otherwise.

The first child had been about ten, had lived all his life as a Nomad, had been very well supplied with the proper hangups for Nomad existence, and had been an extremely disruptive influence in the Surplus classes. Kahvi had always suspected that the teachers themselves had collaborated in the parents' successful effort to recapture him. Since becoming a Nomad herself, she had always hoped to meet that family.

The other child, also a boy, had been only about three, but even he had had well-developed Nomad habits to bother the Surplus teachers. As far as Kahvi knew, he might be still in the Hill.

In any case, she had no intention of allowing her daughter to be taken away, no matter how well intentioned the kidnappers might be. Danna was already well on the way toward good Nomad self-sufficiency, and her mother was sure she would be badly confused by the things the Hillers would try to teach her—especially with all these oxygen-wasters around.

Also, and almost as serious, if the Hillers took

over control of the raft they would for all practical purposes be in control of the Fyn family. Neither of its adult members was prepared to tolerate that; the urge for independence was still strong in what remained of humanity.

Earrin and Kahvi distrusted city-dwellers on principle, and had often talked over possible situations which might threaten child or home.

None of this went through Kahvi's conscious mind at the moment; it was all background to be taken for granted. The current question was how to get to the raft without being noticed, and how to keep control of it after she had reached it. The former was the more pressing; there were various plans already made up to cover the latter, though it remained to be seen whether any of them were practical.

She was a much quicker thinker than her husband, as Earrin himself was ready to admit, and it did not take her long to set up a plan of action. She didn't like it—she was not, in fact, certain that she could do it—but like her husband she executed decisions quickly. Too much time spent thinking could, as she had told the jailbird earlier, be deadly. She had not, as a Nomad, faced enough unexpected situations to realize that lack of thought could be equally so. Right now, dawn could not be far away, and too much light would certainly spoil things.

Still close to the ground, she worked her way around to the south side of the jail. Then, keeping the structure between herself and the cargo pile, she half rose and ran as rapidly as she could southward and a little away from the water. This brought her gradually up the hillside, and presently the jail ceased to provide concealment. However, the vegetation was thicker here, and she dropped back to the ground and crawled quickly straight up the slope. Once over the ridge and a short distance down the other side she felt safe in standing up, and after pausing a moment to get her breath she turned northward again.

Her path brought her fairly close to the fire site where Bones had been captured a few hours before, but very fortunately—her feet were unprotected—not near enough to feel its heat and be tempted into a real investigation.

Opposite the raft she approached the ridge again cautiously, travelling prone and exposing as little as possible of her head above it. Knowing that rapid motion was more likely to catch the human eye than any mere shape, she spent fully two minutes bringing her eyes to the level where she could see the raft and the cargo area.

The two Hillers were still at the latter place, working as they had been ordered. Even at three hundred meters distance and through the rather ripply mask glass they could be seen clearly enough. It was not possible to tell how much attention they were giving to other matters—how well, for example, they might be watching for Earrin—but her plan would take care of that anyway.

If she could carry it out. She had budgeted time for driving herself to the act, but as the eastern sky

grew brighter she began to wonder whether she
had allowed enough. It went against so many
Nomad hangups. She was afraid of fire; it was
dangerous and evil. It destroyed resources, both
real-life and pseudolife which people needed for
survival. It even destroyed structures, unless they
were made of stone—and even those, if the stones
were held by ordinary pseudolife cements. It even
hurt, she knew, though she had never suffered a
burn yet herself.

But these Hillers were a menace. They
threatened the welfare and the lives of Kahvi herself, her husband, and her child, especially the
child. If they got a good look at Kahvi they might
even become a threat to the child still unborn; its
presence was now reasonably obvious, though
Kahvi's figure was basically rather solid. The jailbird she had seen might already be aware of the
newcomer. Worse, these people were oxygen-
wasters, addicts, and therefore even less predict-
able and trustworthy than other Hillers.

And, after all, the fire wouldn't actually *hurt*
them. It wouldn't even damage the jail, of
course—if there had been risk of that, Kahvi could
not have brought herself to start it under any
circumstances. The jail was an oxygen haven,
even with its present overgreat oxygen concentration.

Having convinced herself again that this particular end was worth the proposed means—
though still uneasy about it down inside—she
worked her way back a few meters from the ridge
and set to work. Naturally the fire must not be
allowed to spread any distance, so she tried to

clear every single growth from a large radius and the recognizably explosive ones from an even greater distance around the proposed lighting spot. She was careful not to pile blasters on top of each other, covering them and separating them with less violent growths. By the time she was satisfied, the eastern sky was getting quite bright; there was little more time.

She worked more slowly and hesitantly now, however. Unfastening a couple of straps, she brought her breathing cartridges around in front, and disconnected one of them. It was a cylinder about the size of her forearm, with a valved hose extending from one end. The outer case had been made of "plastic"—a construction tissue of any sort grown by pseudolife—while the organ inside had been grown as a unit.

The oxygen-binder was a scion of one of the last forms of pseudolife to be designed before human culture lost the ability to produce such things from basic materials. Like most such "organisms" it was extremely stable genetically, though mutations sometimes occurred—more accurately cancers, since it was reproduced by culturing a fragment separated from the parent body. Structurally it was a single-thickness sheet of cells so highly involuted that nearly all of them were exposed to the surroundings; the area within the unit totalled many hundreds of square meters. The cells contained an oxygen binding complex similar to, but far more efficient than, hemoglobin; its equilibrium oxygen pressure was about a quarter of a standard atmosphere, changing little through the usual temperature range.

The cartridge fed normally into a bellows-like arrangement intended to permit controlled mixing with ordinary air, now almost entirely nitrogen. The traces of nitrogen oxides in the atmosphere were not filtered out or separated in any other way; they were responsible for the short average life span of Nomads.

Kahvi had found a growth which had a more intimate mixture than most of nitrates and reducers—a sort of super blaster; once or twice she had seen it ignite from impact. This, of course, could not be counted on; the "real" nitro-life, unlike the artificial varieties, mutated almost constantly. Bones had remarked more than once that eating was an endless experiment, though the Nomads had not translated the gestures with just that word.

Kahvi hoped that in a jet of straight oxygen this bit of wood could be expected to fire on impact, though it had not done so in ordinary air when she broke off the branch. She found a smooth stone and placed it beside her spread-out woodpile. Then, holding her breath to conserve the last lungful, she removed her mask and placed the delivery tube of the disconnected cartridge in her mouth. The mask and rebreather bellows were still connected to each other and to the remaining oxygen cartridge. She turned the inside of the mask toward the stone, raised the stick, squeezed the bellows—

And stopped. She couldn't do it. Everything in the way of memories and habit patterns which made Kahvi Mikkonen what she was ordered her arm to stop the swing. For a moment she knelt motionless; then she brought the bellows back to her face, let it fill, and breathed again—the tube from the other cartridge had only diffused oxygen to her mouth, not nearly fast enough to keep her alive for long. The cartridge tissue outgassed to equilibrium very rapidly, but there had to be somewhere for the gas to go. The bellows, diluting it with nitrogen, made a large difference.

"Experiment!" she muttered, using what her Surplus school teachers had regarded as the vilest of words. Then she clenched her teeth, thought of her home and family again, drew another deep breath of diluted oxygen, and tried again.

This time the paralysis came too late to stop the impact, though the blow was far less violent than she had meant. Sparks flew, and the end of the stick took on a crimson glow; she had her fire. She dropped the wood, and quickly replaced her breathing gear. Then, seeing the incandescence spreading rapidly to include the entire branch, she seized it by the still-cold end and threw it into the wood pile.

Then she fled, almost fainting.

It took several minutes for the spreading glow to reach any of the blaster plants, and she was well to the north before the first crimson flash illuminated the view and the accompanying heavy thud reached her ears. She promptly dropped flat again and wriggled toward the top of the ridge, bringing her head up with as much care as before. The people might not be so stupid as to look only at the fire. She was recovering her self-control, though she felt nauseated.

Both workers were running toward the jail,

calling out loudly. As far as Kahvi could tell at
that distance, neither was looking back. She still
played it safe, however, crawling down toward
the water.

She had farther to go than the runners, and they
got to the jail before she reached the water. The
moment they disappeared into the lock pool,
Kahvi got to her feet and ran as fast as she could;
she was safely submerged before the other
oxygen-wasters had donned gear and come outside.

The moon was still visible after a fashion in
spite of the brightening sky. Its image was distorted and swung back and forth by the swell, but
it gave some guide to direction. Kahvi stayed
below the surface entirely—charged breathing
cartridges were much denser than water, and she
needed no effort to stay down—until she felt sure
that she had swum farther out than the raft. Then,
still very carefully, she raised her head. The swell
alternately lifted and lowered her nearly a meter,
but she caught glimpses of shore and raft.

She was still well north of the latter, and somewhat farther from shore. She was tempted to stay
on the surface for easier navigation, but the six
Hillers were now outside the jail. Even though
they were moving rapidly toward the fire—the
crimson glow and rising column of smoke made
her feel sick again for a moment—and seemed to
be paying no attention to any other direction,
Kahvi decided to play it safe and submerged
again. The next time she came up to check she was
almost directly out from the raft, about a hundred
meters, and the people were all out of sight. She

finished her journey on the surface until she had to go down again to get to the entry hatchway. She climbed in as quietly as she could, but it wasn't quietly enough; the child felt the change in motion of the floats.

"Mother, is that you? Where were you? There's another fire, and I'm scared. Should we go out with the buckets again?"

"No, dear. This is just a little fire, and it won't come close. You may watch it or go back to sleep, whichever you want."

"Which will you do?"

"I'll watch for a while. Do you want to come over here with me?"

There was no verbal answer, but the floats changed their rhythm again and a moment later her daughter's tiny form was cuddled against her. No more words were necessary, and Kahvi carefully refrained from using any. Danna helped remove her mother's outdoor gear without asking again where she had been—after all, there was nothing unusual about either of her parents' going out to check anchors or other things even at night. Several silent minutes passed, and Kahvi began to hope that the little one had gone back to sleep.

But she hadn't. She saw the figures in the growing light as quickly as her mother, and felt Kahvi stiffen at the sight.

"Who are those people, Mother? Are they coming here?"

"They may be. Get your outdoor gear on, Dan, but don't connect cartridges until they really come into the water. Be quick."

JANET AULISIO

X

Contretemps, Confused

It was brighter after passing the air lock. The lighting system of the city could not compete with daylight, but was better than moon and comet together. Earrin had intended to emerge from the water very carefully, but realized in time that this would be more likely to attract attention than a casual entrance. As it happened, his attempt at nonchalance was wasted, since no one was inside the cavern which held the air lock. This was hardly surprising in view of the hour, but Fyn still felt relieved.

That lasted for only a moment, until he suddenly realized that he had no real plan of action. The two main needs were obvious: he had come to find the captive native, and he would of course have to get his breathing cartridges recharged. The latter would take care of itself if he could leave them exposed to city air for enough hours, but it would be better to get them into the full-pressure oxygen of a life-support bubble.

How the captive could be found when Fyn had not the slightest knowledge of the city's layout, beyond occasional details mentioned by his wife, was far from obvious. Earrin began to suspect that he was not being very realistic, or even very sensible. Presumably the life support area would be at the top of the city, since it would need sunlight—Kahvi had, in fact, said as much. About all that could be done, therefore, was to take every opportunity he could find of going upward. He started along the first corridor which caught his eye, out of the dozen which opened into the cave.

Within fifteen minutes he was hopelessly lost. The tunnels were not straight, as Bones was to discover some hours later.

However, he kept on. Presumably the higher he got, the smaller would be the city area; it was quite likely that life-support took up the whole top level. He was not using his own air—this would have bothered his conscience as a rule, but at the moment the city owed him—and there were plenty of hours available.

It was not entirely luck which kept him from being identified as an intruder for all those hours. He had come in at a seldom-used lock above the heavily populated levels; and even though most of the people lived and worked out of sight of the sun, the city was mainly active by day and asleep at night. There was nothing like a regular police or guard force. Like the Nomads, the citizens had to follow rather strict natural laws in order to survive, though the laws were not quite the same as those needed outdoors. The city-dwellers had their own standards of righteousness, and a few generations of enforcing these by firmly Nomadding offenders, combined with the fact that it was difficult for social parasites to get away with their life-style for very long in such a confined area, had made police activity superfluous. There were exceptions, of course; crime waves followed by spells of vigilante activity occurred more or less regularly, but Fyn had made his entrance at a relatively safe part of the cycle.

In better light, his outdoor coloration might have caught attention. However, the pseudolife plates which provided illumination were dim by electrical age standards even where they were regularly fed and watered. Elsewhere they sufficed to keep pedestrians from collision.

Fyn, therefore, had no trouble travelling, even though he had no idea where he was going horizontally. It took him more than an hour to find a stairway going up, though he had encountered two heading downward in that time. He judged, correctly, that this was support for his higher-the-smaller hypothesis. The stairway took him up some twenty meters, passing several levels, before it ended and he had to seek another. This didn't take so long to find, but gained him much less height. It did gain him, though he didn't realize it for some time, a follower; a slender, tentacled form which looked like a fish walking on its tail. He never knew just how long it took him to find the air center, but the sun was high when he finally did. Golden daylight, visible at a distance along a new corridor, was in fact the final guide.

By this time he was meeting people fairly often, but no one paid him much attention in the biolit tunnels. His act of nonchalance had been perfected by practice, and he no longer felt the urge to duck into a side tunnel whenever someone appeared ahead. His follower was doing this, so far in time to have avoided notice. There was more system to these upper corridors; the Observer had worked it out, and succeeded in getting back on Earrin's trail each time it had been necessary to hide. Actually the being did not regard the concealment as really essential, but wanted to keep track of Fyn without compromising him.

With the increasing number of people around, Earrin was feeling less and less sure of himself as the minutes wore on. When the sunlight appeared ahead, his spirits revived a little; this had to be the air and food supply region, and he could recharge both air cartridges and stomach in a short time if he weren't recognized in the brighter light. How many attendants would there be on hand? How preoccupied would they be with their routine work? Could anyone come in, eat, and exchange or renew cartridges without any formality? Kahvi had never told him.

His tension mounted again as he approached

the daylit end of the tunnel and a figure appeared there a few meters ahead of him. Fortunately this one, a woman who looked a good deal older than Kahvi, had just been in full sunlight and for the moment could see scarcely anything. She did detect Earrin's presence and nodded indifferently as she passed him, but that was all. That left the man five meters from daylight with no obstacles in sight.

He did not, however, reach full sunlight just then. A sudden shout of surprise in a female voice sounded from behind him and caused him to swing about sharply. A few meters away was the woman who had just passed him; about as far beyond her, another shape was disappearing into a side passageway. The Observer had run out of luck. Fyn, his eyesight already affected by the brightness he had been approaching, was not sure of details, but he saw enough to tell why the woman had shrieked. His first impulse was to get out of sight himself, and he almost turned back toward the end of the tunnel. However, the woman had already seen him; and if there were people in the plant room who had also heard her cry . . .

He came quickly down the tunnel to where the woman was standing. "What's the trouble?" he asked, in a voice whose anxiety was not entirely feigned.

"I saw something—one of the outside animals—duck into that side alley," she replied, in a voice much calmer than the cry of a moment earlier.

"How could that be possible?" asked Fyn. "How

would one get in the city?''

"Don't be silly," was the less than tactful reply.
"They could get in through any air lock. The
mayor insists we can't watch them all and claims
it's dangerous to block any of them up. *I* say it's
more dangerous to leave them open now that we
don't need them all. But what are we to do about
this animal?''

"Why do anything? What harm can he do?"
asked Fyn in what he considered a calm and
reasonable manner. The woman turned sharply
and looked at him carefully for the first time.

"Where were you brought up?" she snapped.
"They're not citizens, and have no right to the
city's air. Are you one of these liberal delinquents
who claim there's more than enough oxygen?''

"But they don't use air. They don't breathe,"
Earrin pointed out.

"How would you know?" the woman peered
more closely.

"I work outside." Earrin made the only possible
answer, at the same time holding up his breathing
mask.

"And how would that tell you anything about
the animals, unless—" she paused, and appeared
to forget her first anxiety for a moment. "Come
back to the light with me." She took him by the
arm and marched him rapidly toward the end of
the tunnel. Earrin, unused to such a forceful personality except when masked by Kahvi's loving
tact, and quite unable to employ violence against
a person, went along. He was still trying to decide
whether he should face recognition as a Nomad or

jerk away, join Bones—who must have been following him after all, it seemed—and face only
suspicion when they reached daylight. He could
only come up with what he considered reasonable
words.

"How could they live outside if they had to
breathe?" he asked. "I thought citizens, even if
they stay indoors all the time, were supposed to
know at least as much as Surplus kids."

"You can skip the insults," was the answer as
she tugged him along even faster. "You can't tell
me that there's anything that doesn't have to
breathe somehow."

"But how do they—" Earrin gave up. This was a
Hiller, and Hillers thought differently, as Bones
sometimes seemed to. Bones, however, was usually rational if one took the time to work out in
detail what he was saying; this seemed different,
somehow.

Out in the sunlight the woman took one look at
him.

"I thought so. Nomad. I suppose you brought
that animal in with you."

"No, Teacher." Earrin was not being funny; old
reflexes had been triggered. "It may have been
following me, but I didn't know about it."

The woman—a rather thin individual of middle
height, with her hair largely gray but neither skin
nor hair showing any trace of the yellow which
went with outdoor life—seemed to accept the
statement. Nomads, as was common knowledge,
did not lie. "Have you seen it before?" she asked.

"I have seen one before, quite often," Fyn

answered carefully. "I did not see this one clearly enough to be sure whether it is the same." He felt a slight twinge of conscience, but was able to convince himself that this was not deceit; this might not be Bones, though the other was supposed to be a prisoner. "Shall we try to catch him and find out?"

"You should get out of the city at once—you can't say *you* aren't breathing out air. Still, if you will promise not to try to get away from me, and to help me if we do catch up with that thing, all right."

"I promise." Fyn wanted, as badly as the Hiller woman did, to get a better look at the native. It seemed most probably that it was Bones, but the more Earrin thought, the more he felt that there had been something different about the fleetingly glimpsed figure.

"All right. Come on." The woman, again taking Fyn's word at face value, led the way back into the tunnel. They approached the cross passage where the native had disappeared and looked around the corner. Nothing but dimly lit stone and darker doorways could be seen. They went along this, checking inside each room as they passed it. For thirty or forty meters there was no conversation; then the woman spoke again.

"Why did you come into the city? Were you planning to steal something?"

"What does that mean?"

"Take something for your own without having made it or paid for it."

"No. I was looking for something, but not to take it."

"Not even air?" the woman sneered. Fyn was a little shocked at the question.

"How can you steal air?" he asked. "I know you regard it as city property, but surely you wouldn't keep it from anyone for that reason. Of course I would have recharged at your air center." His voice made no secret of his feeling about the matter.

"That is stealing. You have no right to do such a thing."

"I don't agree. In the first place, you don't keep air from anyone who needs it. In the second, some of your people made me go with them last night, and use air I would otherwise have replenished from my own source. I think I have a perfect right to a charge at your city's expense. Those people owe it to me."

"They brought you into the city?"

"No." Fyn's habitual truthfulness was in complete charge, though he had some doubt about telling the whole story to this Hiller. "They said they were going to, but I got away from them. They wanted me to do something I did not approve of. If I had gone home they could have caught me again easily, so I came here to recharge."

"And you just came in through the first air lock you found. No one stopped you?"

"No one was around. It was night. I've been trying to find my way around here all day." His interrogator looked at him shrewdly and, he thought, a little more sympathetically.

"You might have charged up with more than air, then," she remarked.

"Of course. Food goes with air, anyway. Or doesn't your food grow on—"

"Oh, yes. Well, maybe if you're helpful with this animal we can supply you with some of both."

"You owe me some already, if there are any new varieties. I haven't been paid for my cargo yet, and the payment was to be at least two new cultures for making air, food, or some structural material." Earrin explained the situation in detail, still omitting mention of Bones and the Fyn family's relations with the being. The woman seemed quite surprised.

"I hadn't heard of such arrangements being made with Nomads," she said. "I know that people sometimes trade with them, and I'd heard that some people were careless enough of the rules to let new varieties of plant survive. I'm very surprised that such materials were actually used. I don't see what anyone would want with copper or glass. I've seen a few tools made of the metal, and of course the roof of the air section has glass in it to let the sunlight in; but surely no one is going to build more air rooms."

"Glass can be used for tools, too," the man pointed out, drawing his knife and handing it to her. She examined it with interest and returned it. Neither thought of any distinction between *tool* and *weapon*.

"Well, I haven't heard of any special want for either of them," the woman finally repeated. "Come on, let's find this creature. Wait—maybe one of us should go back to the stairway. There's only one to this level. That will keep it from getting away. It could circle back and get there ahead of us if we don't; there aren't any dead ends in these tunnels. Again she had to clarify several of her terms to the Nomad.

"I'm not sure I could find the stairway," Earrin admitted. "If you think it should be watched, you'll have to show me the way, or get some more help. Do you think you can take care of the animal if you catch it by yourself?"

She was silent for a short time. "I don't know," she said at last. "Maybe we should stay together."

"I don't believe it would hurt you. I've seen the one I mentioned often enough without ever having trouble with it. Of course, that woman with the group that had me last night was saying terrible things about them—that they ate their own children, and that sort of thing. Is that what bothers you?"

"What woman? Was this the same group you were talking about? I never heard such a story in my life."

Again Fyn spent some time explaining, interrupting the search once more. For some reason, the woman now seemed even more upset than she had been at the first sight of the native. She was wearing a very perturbed expression when he had finished telling about the "Invaders" as described by his recent captors.

"I think I see some of what's going on," she said slowly. Tell me, did any of these people use—well—dirty language."

"Such as what?"

"I—I can't give you any examples. About—you

know—the things which were done to ruin the world." Fyn thought he saw what she meant.

"You mean things like expressions from the Science Myths." Even the word *science* caused the woman to cringe a little, but she managed to answer.

"Yes—that sort of thing."

"I wouldn't say so—not the words, anyway. They did say they were trying to capture the animals they called Invaders to find out how they could be killed. They dodged the words, but what they were planning was certainly—that word you just now didn't like. Calling it something else doesn't change it. They didn't believe the usual story about the way the air changed—"

"It's not a story! That's what happened. People tried to use—that method—to grow more food. It was a way to get more nitrogen, that their food plants needed, into the ground. The nitrogen combined with the oxygen, and there was a lot more nitrogen even then, so—"

"I've heard the details. Many times. The point is that these people don't believe it; they think the Invaders did something to get the oxygen out of the air. They want to change it back, and think they'll have to get rid of the animals first."

"I know now." The woman's face was eloquent with disgust. "They were all pretty young, weren't they?"

"Yes. Middle teens, I'd say—just about grown up."

"That's it. Those delinquents over in Hemenway. But I didn't think they actually meant to *use*

such methods. Most of us thought they were
merely youngsters with the usual no-one-
can-tell-me-what-to-do idea holding on a little
late. I suppose—'' her voice trailed off, and she
was thinking again.

Fyn was almost as surprised as Bones would
have been at the implication that Hillers were
not all one in mind and spirit, but he was better
able than the Observer would have been to believe
it. He knew that the basic anti-Science religion
differed in dogmatic detail from city to city, but
he had never encountered until now a group
which flatly denied it. He resumed the search
along the corridors silently, not wanting to continue the conversation until he had made more
sense of the new information. The woman, whose
name he did not yet know and who, he suddenly
realized, had never bothered to ask for his, seemed
to feel much the same. She checked the rooms on
her side of the tunnel in complete silence for some
minutes.

She had gotten several doorways ahead of him,
the rooms on her side being all single while most
of those on Fyn's were two- and three-chambered
suites. He was just emerging from one of these
into the main tunnel when he glimpsed two figures disappearing into doorways on the other
side, both well ahead of him. The more distant one
was slower moving, and he had no trouble recog-
nizing his partner in the search; the other, seen
more briefly but more closely, was equally easy to
identify. He sprang silently toward the doorway
through which it had vanished.

The creature had seen him, too, and made no attempt to hide further. It waited, just inside the door, out of sight of the woman if she should come back to the corridor.

It was not Bones; that was evident the moment Earrin entered the room. It was not even as tall as the man himself, though its shape was identical with that of the native. Why it was travelling in the tunnels of Great Blue Hill was a mystery. If it had escaped from its captors, who had apparently been in Hemenway if the woman knew what she was talking about, it should be outside by now—or perhaps it was as lost as Fyn himself. He would have liked to ask it, but could think of no way to do so. It might, of course, have learned to understand some spoken words during its captivity, but it probably had the same difficulty in distinguishing phonemes as Bones; and in any case it had no voice with which to answer questions.

Fyn was naturally startled when the tentacles began gesturing meaningfully at him.

"Earrin. I wasn't quite sure it was you at first, but followed you to make certain. Should I keep out of sight, or is it all right for this person you are with to see us together and communicating? And can you help me either to get outside, or to find food in here?"

"Bones! What on earth have they done to you? Never mind, you can explain later—yes, there should be food in the air center, and I can find that. It's not far from here. Come on."

Much of this was of course spoken aloud, and

the woman heard the words from farther along the tunnel. She came back hastily.

"You caught it!" she exclaimed happily. Then her attitude changed abruptly. "Why—you were talking to it! How can you talk to an animal? Did you train it, the way people did when there were other animals in the world?" Then her expression changed from curiosity and amazement to anger. "You have met it before—you *did* know it! You—*lied*—to—me! What kind of Nomad are you? At least we could always believe them!"

Fyn was even angrier. As the woman spoke, he too had jumped to an unbelievable conclusion, but it seemed to be the only one the data permitted. He snarled back, "You filthy hypocrites! So *experiment* is a dirty word, is it? Science is evil, and ruined the world, you say? And the people who use it are delinquents? Don't talk to me about lying. You Hillers have been experimenting on my friend! Come on, Bones, let's go. We'll get your food and my air if we have to knock some of these subhumans down flights of stairs. Then we'll get out of here!"

JANET AULISIO

XI

Experiment, Educational

The spear hurt, and pulling it out hurt a good deal more. Bones expected another flight of the weapons as the process was tried, but the human beings watched with interest as the handling tentacles pulled the long shaft on through and dropped it on the floor. The flow of nearly colorless blood ceased quickly. The Observer body was by no means either immortal or invulnerable, but most of the organs which would be vital to a human being were decentralized. There was no single heart, but hundreds of far smaller pump muscles along the blood vessels; nerve cells used

internal information storage instead of the
human method of coding connections, and travelled freely though the body both in the circulatory system and among the cells of the other tissues. Even muscles were not connected groups of
tissue-forming cells but protean structures which
could change their shapes and regroup as needed.
The Observer muscle could actually *push*.

Bones, therefore, was extremely uncomfortable, but not incapacitated. The fact that such
major damage usually stimulated the long body
to a budding reaction was a nuisance, but not a
catastrophe; buds were sometimes even convenient, if they actually duplicated properly. Usually, of course, they didn't.

The fishlike form's failure to fall down startled
the human witnesses, and a buzz of conversation
broke out.

Bones could not, as usual, understand enough of
the syllables to make any sense, and human facial
expressions had never been very meaningful to
the Observer. It was necessary to wait for overt
actions before the thoughts of these people could
be guessed. The one they had made so far was
mystifying, but was at least a datum to remember.

Until they made another, it seemed reasonable
to eat some more. This would be useful even if it
did not stimulate the witnesses to some informative reaction. Bones removed the bubble from
another planter and reached for the contents. The
reaction, unfortunately, was too quick to allow a
taste of the material; there was a single, sharp

syllable barked by one of the tallest of the people, and six more spears were poised for throwing.

Bones did not have combat-type reflexes, but was a reasonably intelligent being. The basic idea of throwing things at beings whose actions were undesirable was new, but not essentially difficult. The actual execution of it might take practice—Bones suspected that making the spear which had already been thrown return point first to its senders would be more difficult than it appeared; but some things could be thrown without worrying about their travel attitude.

The planter was heavy, but not too heavy. Two strong tentacles lashed out, and the box of dirt and plants went flying toward the spearsmen. Two of them had time to launch their weapons, while the other four dropped theirs and ducked, in one case too slowly. More spears were raised. Bones, who had had no trouble dodging the pair just thrown once it was obviously the thing to do, reached for and raised another planter.

The voice which had given orders before sounded again, this time in a monosyllable that Bones was able to understand.

"Stop!"

Bones stopped, not because of the word but because of its effect on the others. Spears were lowered, and their holders were looking at the speaker; even the Observer could tell that they were waiting for more instructions—that the one who had called out was for some reason the controlling mind of the group.

The speech went on, but lapsed into incom-

prehensibility as far as Bones was concerned.
How much information was being conveyed, why
the leader had stopped the violence—there was no
way to tell. If only Earrin or Kahvi, or even little
Danna, had been there—

No use in wishing; it was less useful than inference, or even than guessing. Watching what the
people did was all that could be done now.

The speaker finished. His listeners seemed relaxed, and divided their attention between him
and the Observer; they showed no signs of further
violence as far as the latter could judge.

Only two of the human beings were doing anything. These moved slowly and steadily toward a
table not very far from Bones. Neither carried a
weapon or anything else. Their slow, very controlled actions captured the Observer's attention
more and more completely as the seconds passed.

Both the people were much smaller than usual,
though not nearly as small as Danna—they were
about the height of the other Observer unit which
had been in the prison. Earrin or Kahvi would
have guessed them as being thirteen or fourteen
years old; Bones had no basis for judgement. Both
were males, another fact unknowable and unimportant to the nonhuman.

They stopped two or three tables away from the
tall watcher, and removed a light cover from a
glass tank which covered most of the top of the
furnishing. One of them dipped in with a fabric
net which interested Bones greatly; it was the first
woven material the Observer remembered seeing.
The pocket of the tool went into a layer of milky-

looking, thin mud which filled the lowest third of the tank; it was withdrawn, held to drain for a moment, and brought toward Bones.

The latter wondered whether food were being offered, but as the net continued to drip the upper part of its contents cleared to a snowy white; and when it came close enough the nature of the substance was clear—too clear.

It was a fluffy pile of the glass splinters which had made so effective a trap back at the fire site. For the first time, Bones noticed that all the human beings were wearing sandals.

Evidently satisfied that the material had been recognized, the small human being walked toward a nearby door and began to spread the stuff over the floor in its area. The other youngster had dipped up another load, and was doing the same at another door. It took no great deductive power to see what was happening, but there was nothing obvious the Observer could do about it. The larger beings still held their spears. Within five minutes, every door in the room was unapproachable, as far as Bones or any bare-footed human being was concerned.

The Observer was interested, but not worried. This was certainly a better method of restraint than the bars, except for one factor. It was fascinating that the people seemed not to have considered that factor; unless and until they did, other matters could be studied.

The tank from which the glass had come, for example. There were several more like it, some containing layers of gray mud like the first, others

with lumps of spongy tissue in various stages of
solution. It was obvious enough that the glass
spicules were being grown in some form of
pseudolife, and the supporting tissue was merely
dissolved away when mature. Earrin would be
interested, though he would probably have no use
for the material.

Now the human beings put their spears down,
except for half a dozen who left the room with
theirs. Those who remained set frantically to
work. Some collected the fragments of the planter
Bones had thrown, others picked up, very carefully, the bits of tissue from the growths it had
contained. The people who had been hit by the
missile were among those who had left, some of
them still limping. The tissue was carefully
placed in soil in several trays which were brought
in from another room. Some of these were set up
on empty tables, others carried through one of the
doors out of sight. The planters from which Bones
had eaten were examined carefully, and their cov-
ers replaced. All this was fairly obvious in purpose; Bones had seen Earrin and Kahvi carry out
similar routine hundreds of times in the past few
years. The culture, whatever it was, in the planter
which had been smashed was being salvaged; the
others were being checked for possible infection.
There were always nitro-life spores in the air, even
in a well-sealed environment like a city. Important plants such as air and food producers had to
be kept protected, and divided as far as possible so
that no single infection would destroy an entire

resource. The trays Bones had uncovered would be watched with special care for some days.

During all this, the small individuals who had spread the glass simply stood and watched the nonhuman. Bones suspected that they were much younger than the rest, and had begun to wonder whether a communication effort might be worth while. Danna had apparently found it much easier than her parents to learn Bones' tentacle gestures while the code was being perfected; her signal vocabulary was not as great as her parents' so far, but what she knew she had learned much faster. Perhaps this was a quality which went with the more recently budded of the species. It seemed worth trying.

The youngsters were cooperative, watching the motions of Bones' tentacles and, after a while, seeming to get the basic idea and trying to imitate them with waving and posturing of their own arms and fingers. No real transfer of information was accomplished, however; the primary result was the total focussing of Bones' attention on the two beings. This, it turned out, was an error—though the results might have been the same even if the Observer had really been observing.

Even the pain of the spear wound had been forgotten for the moment, when suddenly two nooses settled over Bones' head and tightened below the eyes. They could not get lower than the upper handling tentacles, and these appendages reacted at once, whipping upward and trying to flip the loops of fiber away; but the human crews

pulled hard from opposite directions until the
ropes were cutting painfully into the tough, rubbery flesh. Bones could not, of course, have been
strangled, and the major parts of the circulatory
system of the fishlike body were too deeply located to be blocked this way; but the long form
could and did feel pain. For the time the Observer
was completely helpless.

The youngsters, apparently as startled as
Bones, uttered cries of surprise and what the Fyns
would have recognized as indignation; they had
been getting interested in the embryonic conversation. There was a sharp argument between
them and one of the older beings, which ended
with the youngsters leaving the room sulkily.
They looked back as they went, watching as the
tall form was dragged over to a door, the floor in
the neighborhood swept carefully, and the prisoner moved through it. Bones did not see them
again.

Once in the corridor outside, travel stopped
briefly. The nooses were loosened a little, Bones'
eyeballs relaxed into their proper shape, and their
vision began to come back. Another noose was
applied near the other end of the fishlike form, at
the narrowest part just above the flukes. Two
more followed at the same place; then the upper
ones were removed completely. Bones, analyzing
the situation, could recognize that there was no
immediate chance of escape. The three ropes were
held by three men, standing in three different
directions; any one of them could jerk the support
from under the Observer with no trouble at all.

Untying one of the nooses, even if it could be managed, would be futile, and there certainly was no way to work on all of them at once. It appeared that the men this time felt it would be easier to let their captive provide his own transportation.

Of course, the Observer was in no great hurry to escape, though choosing and managing one's own actions was always preferable. Food needs had been supplied for the time being, and unless the same prison as before were on the schedule there should be new things to learn.

Since there was a fair chance that it *would* be the same prison, however, Bones gave thought to methods of escape as the party resumed its journey.

Ropes were slow to untie, but they could be cut quickly. Did any of these people have a knife? The light was poor for human vision, but not for the Observer's great eyeballs. Outdoor workers, like Nomads, always carried tools; but this might not be so usual inside the city.

Apparently it wasn't. Of the ten people in the party, eight were carrying nothing; indoor garments were scanty enough to leave no doubt about this. Of the two with cases or bags which might possibly contain knives, both were at the far ends of ropes attached to Bones, and seemed determined that the slack in those ropes be kept at an absolute minimum. Once, experimentally, the Observer made a sudden move as though to spring into an intersecting tunnel. The resulting horizontal position, achieved with no perceptible delay, was no surprise. The people provided no help in

getting up, but did not interfere; carrying that
weight was still no part of their plan if it could be
helped. Bones did nothing more which might be
construed as an effort to leave, but filed some data
very carefully. One of the men had been notice-
ably slower than the other two in putting tension
on his rope, though he had coordinated well with
the others in controlling the direction of Bones'
fall.

They did not, after all, go back to the original
prison. To Bones' surprise the party finally came
to an air lock. After donning outdoor equipment
from open shelves which lined the walls near the
pool, they took their captive outdoors. For the
moment, this completely baffled Bones.

About three hundred meters east and slightly
downhill from the air lock was a clearing—a real
clearing, with the ground almost completely bare.
Not even the usual nitro slime was present, except
in a few patches. The people led Bones to the
center of this area.

Then one of them approached, taking from her
belt one of the bags which the Observer had hoped
might contain a knife. As the youngsters had done,
she brought it close to her captive and made it
obvious that it contained more of the hellish bits
of glass. Then, accompanied by another member
of the group with the other bag, she began walking
around the edge of the clearing scattering the stuff
over the ground. They made several circuits, and
when the bags were empty the soil in a ring fully
three meters wide was, as far as Bones was concerned, untouchable. The sandalled people now

walked out of the clearing. The three who were holding the ropes dropped the ends and started off with the rest, but a sharp voice uttered several syllables. They came back, detached the ropes from Bones, and took them away.

It was close to midday; many hours had passed since the two Observers had fled the cell. Bones wondered what had become of the other unit—not the other *one*; no Observer could think of another as a different entity. They were all parts of one Self.

There were plenty of other things to wonder about, too, and only inferences for answers— better than nothing, but not much better. Certainly not to be compared with Knowledge. Bones was very much in the position of a human being of the Age of Pleasure, surrounded by attractive and complaisant members of the opposite sex, but restrained from all action. The Tantalus legend was also appropriate, though different appetites were involved.

The tentacular legs under the long body were capable of far more rapid running than would have seemed possible to their incredible slenderness, but jumping was another matter. Bones did consider this briefly, but decided that landing on the glass would be enough worse than walking on it to make the risk unacceptable. The ropes were gone—some people obviously thought more rapidly than others—and the slow-reacting person was gone too; the native regretfully filed what had seemed a promising plan.

By this time the whole situation was starting to

make sense. These people were, simply and rationally, trying to find out more about Bones. It was a perfectly sensible thing—just what an Observer would have done. Cooperation was obviously in order. It was too bad the communication effort with the young ones had been interrupted, and it was hard to see why. Did the people have some quicker method than the sound code, after all, for getting information? If not, why were they so willing to delay? Tantalizing mystery again, and again with nothing but inference possible for a solution so far. Unsatisfactory. Best to assume that this *was* a test, presumably of Bones' ability to get out of this situation, and pass it as quickly as possible.

Digging is very difficult with tentacles, but not impossible. The soil covering the bedrock here was shallow, but might suffice. Bones began to scrape it together and carry it to the narrowest part of the glass barrier. The splinters were easy enough to see by daylight, though the native would not have noticed them without experience.

The original idea was to cover a pathway a meter or so wide across the danger strip, but it quickly became clear that there was not enough dirt for this. The Observer changed the plan to a better and quicker one, that of covering only a few small patches and being careful to step exactly on these while departing. It worked perfectly.

Six human beings were waiting just inside the
          They had the decency to carry Bones back
               glass. One of them carried a broom,
with.   .ch she scattered the dirt from the pro-

tected areas. Another person had a bag of the splinters, and renewed the places which Bones and broom had made safe.

Without thinking, the Observer snatched the broom from its wielder, dashed across the clearing, and began to sweep a path to the outside. If the people had had to go around, this might have worked; but their feet were protected, and they could run across the glass without having to clear a way. Once more Bones was carried back, and the swept area restored to deadliness.

So far the contest had been conducted very politely, with neither side using violence. Bones was more than ever convinced that the whole thing was a test, and still felt cooperative if slightly impatient.

This attitude was modified on the second carry when one of the people, accidentally or otherwise, dropped the heavy end of his load onto the glass area. Once again the Observer felt agony much too great to be compatible with sympathy. For a moment the temptation to hurl the nearest human beings off their feet and onto the glass almost won out; but the realization that they were intelligent beings in some ways comparable to Observers, however different in detail, throttled the impulse. The glass this time was at the upper end of a fin and adjacent body, and could be reached with handling tendrils, so Bones ignored the test for a while and concentrated on removing the stuff. The injuries already sustained had, as expected, started the budding reaction, and nothing could be done about that; but there was no reason to suffer more pain than necessary.

By the time the glass was gone and the pain reduced to a dull ache, the sun was well down in the west. Bones had decided to make no more attempts by daylight, in spite of the risk that people might take their test subject indoors for the night. This might even be helpful, if the same individuals held the ropes. Even if they didn't, a chance of using the earlier plan might present itself; if this happened before they reached the air lock, the situation would be perfect. The moon would not rise for some hours after sunset, and the comet of course would be four hours later still.

So Bones let night fall without giving th experimenters the pleasure of another contest. For some time after dark it looked as though the experiment were to run through the night—quite reasonably, the Observer considered—but at last there came a sound of human conversation from the direction of the air lock. Bones got "afoot"—the great body did need rest at times—and waited tensely.

This silhouetted the tall form against the starlit sky, and there was more sound from the opposite direction. It was the quick intake of a human breath, followed by the exclamation, "Bones!" in a voice which even the native could recognize.

"Bones!" Kahvi repeated. "Come on, quickly! The Hillers are coming, and they plan to hurt you—to kill you if they can! Come this way!"

Bones, unfortunately, could do nothing of the sort. The glass was in the way. This was bad enough, though it seemed unlikely that the Hillers could actually kill the rather resilient Observer body; but there was something worse. The woman was approaching. With her unshod feet she would be as vulnerable to the glass as Bones—perhaps more so, considering the thin human skin. The Observer gestured frantically for her to keep back, but the detailed signals simply could not be made out in the darkness. She would be into the splinters in a few seconds; and now it could be seen that little Danna was with her.

XII

Menace, Misunderstood

The wait was short; the approached figures entered the water without a pause. Kahvi had been collecting spare cartridges by touch; now she added some slices of beef and bags of milk from the food plants, and wrapped the former in tissue. Some of the Hillers were swimming, now.

"All right, Dan," she whispered. "Plug in. Into the water, and hold onto my harness. I'll swim, you stick!" The child gave her mother's arm a silent squeeze of assent, and they slipped quietly into the sea together. Kahvi headed north as fast as she dared. The drag on her harness was lighter than it might have been; evidently the little one still wanted to feel useful, and was swimming with her feet. They stayed as close to the bottom as possible, keeping the wavering moon behind and to their left, though it was increasingly hard to see in the growing daylight.

Presently the water became too shallow for swimming. Kahvi pulled Danna around in front of her, touched the child's breathing mask in a gesture for silence, turned her face down, and then, indicating that they should stay side by side, began to crawl slowly and carefully onward. Their course soon took them out of the water.

They had reached the nearer of the Sayre islets. It was only a couple of hundred meters from the anchorage, but was heavily overgrown with all sorts of vegetation and offered excellent concealment. Kahvi did not intend to remain here indefinitely; she was hoping that the Hillers, not finding her at the raft, would assume she had gone toward the city. There were no air sources in this direction. She would get back home by darkness; there was enough air in their cartridges to last through the day. After nightfall she would move the raft behind the islets; Earrin would know where to look for it, and it could be hoped that the Hillers would not guess.

Well into the jungle and away from the water, the two fugitives constructed a comfortable nest from the abundant vegetation and settled down. The mother wanted to sleep, but Danna wanted explanations. Kahvi made the situation as clear as possible, keeping her voice to a whisper which barely got through her mask, but didn't try to explain what might happen to Danna if the Hillers caught her; considering Bones' share in her upbringing, it was conceivable that the child's curiosity would override her caution. She had occasionally expressed curiosity about what it was like in cities.

By the time the conversation was finished it was full daylight, though the sun was not quite up. The moon was almost invisible in the golden sky, and the comet had faded entirely from view. Kahvi stretched out to sleep, after whispering to her daughter, "You should sleep if you can, because there'll be a lot to do later. I know it's pretty bright for sleeping, though. If you can't, at least stay close to the nest while I do. We'll have to be rested before the sun goes down—maybe sooner." With that, the mother closed her eyes and relaxed as completely as possible.

The child soberly examined everything in sight. She looked closely at slime-saturated soil and plant-furred rocks, pulled branches, leaves, and bark from the larger growths surrounding the nest and compared them minutely, and even stood up to see what could be seen at greater distances. She was careful, however, to make sure that she could not be seen from the south; she kept as close as possible to a densely-growing cordage bush taller than she was, peeping cautiously out from behind it. She even ventured a few meters from the nest, but obeyed the injunction to keep in sight of her mother. Her training had been effective. She found several objects, mostly pseudolife

forms, which were new to her; these she collected
carefully and brought back to the nest for her
mother to explain when she woke up. One was an
Evolution plant, the artificial organism which
produced enzymes affecting the stable structures
of most of the other pseudo forms. It was this
fabrication which made it possible for humanity
to continue to manipulate the artificial organisms
in a rough trial-and-error fashion long after
human technological culture had decayed, just as
some of the "countercultures" of an earlier time
had been able to use and even maintain and repair
motor vehicles while not being able to make them.

If Kahvi had seen that plant she would have left
the island at once; she would have realized that it
was not a safe hiding place. The thing itself was
not dangerous to human biochemistry, but its
presence would have told her the Hillers would be
around. The Evolution plant never grew wild; it
needed too much attention. It was completely
symbiotic with the present human culture.

But Kahvi never saw it. She didn't have time
after waking up.

It was midafternoon when Danna was
awakened by the sounds of people crashing
through the jungle. Her reaction was the right
one; she squeezed her mother's bare shoulder
with one hand, and laid a finger of the other over
Kahvi's mask where it covered the mouth. The
woman was awake almost at once, and immediately grasped the situation. Nodding approval at the child, she rose cautiously and peered
through the bushes in the direction of the sound.

This was from the west, the nearest mainland, rather than the south from which the fugitives had come. It seemed possible to escape back toward the water, but at first she considered the chances of getting submerged unseen to be too small to be worth taking. The alternative, however, was to keep hidden in the jungle; and neither of them could be sure of moving around quietly enough for that to be practical policy. There was no way to conceal the nest, and even if these people were not already hunting for the fugitives, they would be once that was seen. If that did occur, it behooved Kahvi and her child to be well away from the site, preferably with a broad choice of travel plans.

So the water was the best bet after all. Again warning Danna to silence, Kahvi led the way slowly and carefully back along the path they had made earlier. Behind them, voices and snapping branches grew louder—the Hillers were certainly not being subtle about their doings. It was tempting to go faster and get under water as soon as they possibly could, but the woman knew that a splash would be easy for the Hillers to distinguish among their own noises. She held herself to the slow pace, and Danna, frightened as she was, stayed with her.

When the water was hip-deep on the child, they stopped and readjusted their burdens so as to give the little one a free hand with which to hold her mother's harness. Then the woman lowered herself slowly and carefully until she was as nearly submerged as possible, crawled until the water was a little deeper, and finally began to swim. Within a few meters they were both submerged, and Kahvi could relax a little.

She was heading back toward the raft; there was nothing else to do, though she had planned to wait until dark. A trip to the north around the peninsula to reach some of the west side jails would be possible, but risky given limited air and the child. If they could get back home without having to risk discovery by surfacing they would have more resources and a chance to think. Presumably they would also have warning of the approach of another search party. Finding such a goal under water would not be easy, but they could spend hours in the search if necessary. The sun was well up and would provide directional guidance, and the water depth would mean something. Kahvi was in no sense a professional diver, but in the earth's present condition the difference between air and water was more one of seeing than of breathing: Danna thought of underwater as the part of outdoors where it was hard to see.

The biggest problem was judging attained distance, but Kahvi felt sure that if they did not get too far out they should encounter raft or anchors easily enough. The gesture language was specific enough to let her tell Danna the plan, and presently she allowed the child to let go and swim separately a few meters to her right to help in the search. She could be trusted not to show herself above the surface.

It was in fact the child who encountered an anchor line. She grasped it and waved eagerly to her mother. Kahvi responded, swam over, and led the way along the cord to the raft itself. Leaving Danna huddled on the bottom in the shadow of the floats, the woman cautiously approached the entrance, placed her feet on the bottom, and slowly stood up.

Nobody could be seen inside the tent. The floats were bobbing in a heavy swell, and she could not tell by their heights whether any of them concealed extra weight. Finally, still unsure, she climbed cautiously up into the tent. Keeping her head below the general level of the air and food plants, she crawled slowly around among their trays checking the whole interior of the structure. Finally sure that there was no one else inside, she lifted her head slowly to see whether anyone was in sight on or toward the shore.

There was, rather closer than she had expected. The head and very broad shoulders of a man seated at the shoreward end of the raft caught her eye and prevented her from rising far enough to see the rest of him. He was looking to his right, toward Sayre, at the moment. Kahvi felt an internal fluttering which might have been the baby but was probably her own nervous system readjusting. How could this fellow have failed to see the fugitives when they entered the water at the island? How had she failed to see him? The distance was only two hundred meters. Of course her own attention had been focused in the opposite direction, and maybe Hiller mask windows were even worse than those she was used to. Still . . .

Why was he outside? It would have been smarter to hide in the tent if he wanted to intercept Earrin or Kahvi. Had he been inside? If so, he must know about Danna, whose toys and spare outdoor harness could not be mistaken for anything but what they were. Perhaps he had been inside, made the discovery, and decided to wait on the deck so that the Fyns might not guess what he had learned.

There was no point in theorizing or guessing; long association with Bones had made the woman almost as impatient with speculation as the Observer. The important thing was for her and Danna to get away again unobserved. This meant a long underwater journey—the trip around the peninsula would have to be risked now. Going south was pointless; the shore curved east, and they would be in view wherever they emerged for several kilometers unless they happened to find some small creek. That would be asking for too much from luck.

Should they take more supplies? No. There were no more charged air cartridges, and they already had food to last as long as their air. Besides, crawling about the tent picking meat and drink pods from the plants would be asking for the attention of the guard.

As she reached this conclusion, Kahvi saw the fellow suddenly lean forward. She tensed; was he about to leave the raft? Or come inside? Then the anxiety was replaced by a mixture of relief and sympathy. The fellow was actually removing his mask, and his torso and shoulders were heaving unmistakably. Every few seconds he held his mask to his face—he was evidently not entirely out of control—but it was evident why he had not seen the fugitives and why it might even be safe to collect more food. The unfortunate fellow was seasick.

Firmly quelling the reflex urge to help—there should obviously be someone nearby to manage the mask if he did lose control—Kahvi eased back into the water. After all, if these Hiller oxygen-junkies were such idiots as not to have one of their own people on hand—she stopped that thought firmly. She knew perfectly well that jobs had to be done and chances sometimes taken to do them. This Hiller was doing his own job and taking his own chances; good breath to him. Still, her job was to take care of Danna and Earrin.

So she told herself as she swam back to the child, but she was uncomfortable about it. Not quite as uncomfortable as after she had lighted the fire, but queasy enough. Conflict-of-duty questions had been few for Kahvi Mikkonen since she had been a Nomad, and they bothered her. Maybe Earrin, when she found him or he got back to them, would be a help; he was the sort who could keep from worrying over things that couldn't be mended. On the other hand, she might not be able to bring herself to tell him about the fire. He had been an understanding and tolerant teacher in the early months of her Nomad life—otherwise she would never have developed the affection for him which she had—but even he must have a limit somewhere, and lighting fires might be beyond it.

With Danna swimming close beside her this time, Kahvi hugged the bottom closely as they moved away from the raft. She headed almost east for a time. She was not going to risk going between Sayre and the mainland; the water was

deep enough, but there was the obvious risk of
running into the search party on its way back
from the island. Since they might also be intend-
ing to look over the smaller one farther north,
there was at least a kilometer and a half to swim
around this. Danna, her mother was sure, could
make the distance as long as they went slowly
enough. The water was warm enough so that even
the little one's big surface-to-volume ratio offered
no risk of chilling. All Earth's water was warm
these days, except next to the still-vanishing pole
caps. The acid seas had given off most of their
dissolved carbon dioxide, and carbonate minerals
were busily doing the same; greenhouse effect was
warming the planet. Nitrogen dioxide, blocking
some of the incoming radiation, was slowing the
process, but where it would end no one could tell.
Fortunately for general peace of mind, no human
being left on the planet had any idea of the process; and it had not even occurred to Bones.

By keeping in less than four meters of water, the
two were able to contour-chase around the islands, but they were both extremely hungry by
the time Kahvi judged they had come far enough.
Danna had not yet learned how to eat under water, though the Nomad masks permitted this. The
woman did not consider this a good time for a
lesson in the art, since an error in coordination
might have forced them to surface in order to get
water out of Danna's mask, so she had not eaten
either.

As it turned out, they had come rather farther
than necessary. They came up at the mouth of the
cove on the northwestern tip of the peninsula,

where Bones had decided the night before not to
attempt landing. Kahvi, aware that the searchers
might have come this far but considering it most
unlikely, chose to take the chance. The two swam
ashore, got quickly out of sight in the dense vegetation, and settled down to eat.

The sun was now well past the meridian. Danna
was very tired from the swim, and Kahvi decided
that time had to be taken to rest, though they
would have to find a jail or some other oxygen
source before too many hours. They didn't build a
nest this time; there was a fluff organism large
enough to keep the small body off the ground, and
the child curled up in this, while her mother
scouted the area for useful plants. The peninsula,
or at least this part of it, seemed to have been
visited by people who had allowed many kinds of
pseudolife to take hold; Kahvi wondered whether
this had been intentional. She would have been
much more certain if she had seen the one which
Danna had found on Sayre. There were tissue
producers of a dozen kinds at least; a gigantic
block of the Newell material from which the Fyns
made their raft floats, the transparent stuff which
was used for roofs, even the highly specialized
material from which breathing cartridges were
loaded. At present, of course, this was empty;
Danna, waking up at last, was able to pick up logs
of it larger than herself. She amused herself
throwing one of these around while her mother
explained the uses of the different growths.

"Do you think you could find these again if we
wanted them?" Kahvi asked at length.

The child looked thoughtful. "Where will we be

when you ask? I don't know where home is, right now."

Kahvi laughed. "Good for you! Mother wasn't thinking, was she? Here, let me show you." Even with air shortage threatening, the child had to learn, and a few minutes could be budgeted for a mapping lesson. Danna caught on quickly, and after a few minutes study of the diagrams Kahvi scratched in the earth, she was able to point out the direction to the raft and even give a fair description of how long it might take to get there. Very satisfied with themselves and each other, the two resumed their journey.

There was only a small amount of food left. Kahvi rolled it into a single pack of tissue and fastened this to her harness. She was still fatigued, and even Danna had not slept very long; but the woman let the child straddle her shoulders, after readjusting cartridges and breathing lines to make room, and set off again a little west of south. The bulk of Great Blue Hill loomed three kilometers away in that direction, but she was using this as a guide rather than a goal. She planned to follow the ridge which led south along the peninsula—the same one which overlooked the anchorage—high enough to get a good view of the land in hope of spotting jails, but not high enough to be seen from the anchorage itself or the islands.

The choice of route was unfortunate, since it led close to the fire site which Bones had found. Kahvi saw this, and once again decided that the search for air could be postponed a few more minutes to examine this curiosity. The Bones trait was contagious, at least to intelligent people.

The contents of the fire pit had now reduced themselves to white ash which would not have glowed visibly even at night, but some heat could still be felt. Kahvi realized as Bones had done that this must be the site of the fire which had imperilled the nearby jail. She also saw that the stone wall which had been around it must have been artificial, and had to examine it closely even though it was obviously not an oxygen source—at least not any longer. She put Danna down, advising her to rest, but made no mention of the danger of appearing at the top of the ridge.

The child, tired as she still was, wanted to make sure that the ideas she had gotten from the map were right. If so, she judged, she would be able to see the raft from the elevation only a few dozen meters away; and without Kahvi's noticing, she headed quietly in that direction. The vegetation here was too sparse to hide either from the view of the other, and the girl felt perfectly safe.

Inevitably, she encountered the same bed of glass slivers which had trapped Bones. Her scream brought Kahvi on the run. Her reflexes were good, and she placed only one foot in the danger area; she managed to stop before the other was injured, and even held back the cry of pain which almost escaped her lips. She snatched up the child and retreated several meters, ignoring the agony in her left foot until she felt they had reached a safe distance from whatever was causing the pain.

Then she put Danna down gently, sank to the ground herself, and fainted.

JANET AUUSIO

XIII

Peregrination, Painful

It was pain that caused the faint, and pain that
brought back consciousness; Kahvi was out of action only a few seconds. Danna's shrieks had
ceased, and the mother's awakening was completed by the realization that the child had torn
her mask off—it had interfered with the deep
breaths needed for the cries. The little chest was
still heaving, but the lips had already turned blue.
Again Kahvi's own pain was forgotten. She
snatched up the discarded breathing gear,
squeezed the bellows to empty it of outside air,
replaced the mask on the child's face, and pulled

the bellows open again to fill it with straight oxygen from the cartridges. It was no longer possible to see the lips, but the convulsive gasping grew quieter and in a minute or so the still unconscious girl was breathing normally.

Kahvi, her terror reduced to a bearable fear, examined her own foot. Like Bones, she had no trouble identifying the cause of the pain. In full sunlight the slivers were easy to see, and for the most part easy to withdraw. Their shape made them easy to get hold of; they were not simple, straight splinters, but caltrops, their four ten-millimeter points directed tetrahedrally. No matter how they landed on the ground, one point was always upward. The other three provided a good stand on the ground and, fortunately, a good handle for pulling the things out where they protruded from the skin, provided they had not broken off. Two or three had done this, and Kahvi was still working on the last of these when Danna began to regain consciousness.

The mother instantly turned her attention to relieving the child's pain. Pulling out the Hiller-spikes, as the woman had mentally dubbed them, did not hurt very much; the real torture came when they were pushed in. Danna, once she was fully conscious and had been made to understand what had happened, was able to help with the removal.

She had been far more seriously hurt than her mother, however. Both feet had gotten into the trapped area, and she had then fallen down, so that both hands and much of her right arm, leg, and side were involved. They removed nearly forty of the things; Kahvi's foot had contained only seven.

Danna, with her mother's help, got to her feet at last and walked gingerly around. There were still tears behind her mask, but the sobbing had stopped. It was obvious that she was still in pain, but the pride of self-sufficiency and self-command which her parents had tried so hard to instill was taking over.

"Can you walk all right, now?" Kahvi asked. Danna gave an affirmative nod. "Good. I'll still carry you for a while, because I know you're tired and your feet are sore, but I had to be sure that you *can* go by yourself if you have to. Now, remember. We're looking for a place to get air—air and food, but mostly air. You know the jail. What we'll most likely find is something that looks like that, though maybe bigger or smaller. It will probably be on a river—"

That word had to be explained. So did the reason why they were travelling near the top of the ridge when what they sought should be in a valley. So did what they would have to do if they didn't find a jail. It was some minutes before Kahvi could swing the little one up to her shoulders again and resume their journey.

She was rather proud of herself: It had been a temptation to denounce the Hillers as a tribe of subhuman, torturing savages and murderers. Her anger at the people who had set out those hellish bits of glass was still at white heat, but she had not passed it on to her daughter—though she knew

that if she met a Hiller at this moment her normal
hangups against violence might not hold up.
There would actually be pleasure in tearing the
mask from his—or her—face and throwing it as
far as possible, and watching the creature run
after it, and stagger, and fall, and die as Danna
almost had. It might even be pleasant to watch
such a person roll on ground covered with the
same bits of glass he had obviously intended for
use against other people. To hear him shriek as
Danna had shrieked—to watch him tear off his
own mask in agony, as her own little one had
done—

Kahvi suddenly had to put the child down and
open the eating flap of her mask. For two or three
minutes she was very sick, while the child
watched in uncomprehending sympathy.

When she stood up again, the mask once more in
place, her mind as well as her stomach had been
cleared, but she felt depressed. She usually en-
joyed looking at things—at hills and trees and
plants, at clouds and sky; she had never seen a
green Earth, but regarded the multicolored one
she knew as beautiful. Now, however, she could
not appreciate it. It was not just the realization
that habits of human behavior formed such a thin
skin over antihuman urges; there was more material fear. She could not appreciate any beauty as
she walked. Travelling was not just walking;
every step had to be taken with care. She was
unlikely to see the Hiller-spikes even if she walked
bent over with her face as close as possible to the
ground. This meant that every step had to be

taken cautiously, feeling for the slightest twinge
of pain, ready to pull back at once before weight
was put on the foot.

She had no way of telling where the Hillers
might have set other traps. The only obvious quality about the first one was that it lay between the
fire site and the raft. Had it been intended to keep
people—barefooted people—away from the fire,
or from the structure which had been destroyed
by the fire? If so, there might be no more traps; but
there was no way to be sure, and she could take no
risks—certainly not with Danna; so she went very,
very slowly. The delay was irritating, and the irri-
tation gradually brought back the subhuman
thoughts about Hillers . . .

They followed more nearly the way Bones had
been carried than the route taken by her husband.
Hemenway, the nearest of the Blue Hills, was the
eminence Kahvi was now taking as a reference
point. She knew that the city extended underground from Little Blue Hill on the west to
Hemenway and Houghton on the east; unlike her
husband, she knew the location of many of the air
locks, and knew that she could certainly find one
of these if no jail turned up—though she certainly
hoped to renew air and food somewhere outside
the city.

She might, if these had been her only object,
have headed for the west side of the city where she
did know many of the jails; but she had heard
enough while eavesdropping to make Hemenway
her goal. They had wanted to take Earrin there; he
had apparently escaped on the way there; and

while he might have gone anywhere afterward,
that still seemed the best place to start looking for
him. Unfortunately, none of the contingency
plans they had so often amused themselves by
concocting had managed to cover any situation
much like this one; and well as she knew him,
Kahvi had been quite unable to guess what her
husband might now be up to.

The top of Hemenway was about a kilometer
and a half from the fire site and glass trap, so there
was in fact little chance to get far from Earrin's
actual trail. They encountered the jail to which
her husband's captors had been leading him, and
after some hesitation Kahvi checked the interior,
found it empty, and rested there briefly; but of
course there was no sign of Earrin in the building.
They had passed the point where he had escaped,
but Kahvi had none of the experience needed to
recognize any clues which might have been on the
ground.

She had no hesitation in eating from the food
growing in the jail, or in exchanging her used
cartridges for full ones. The rest was shorter than
either of them liked, and Danna could not see why
they had to go on after finding the food and air her
mother had said they needed. She was outspoken
about this, and Kahvi had to take more time to
explain.

"We can't stay here, because some of the City
people come here sometimes. Remember, we
don't want them to find you."

"But why can't we hide a little way off, and
come back whenever we need air?"

"Maybe we will, but there's something else we want to find."

"What's that?"

"Your father. I think these people may have taken him, so we'll have to get him back just as he and I would get you back if they took you." Danna accepted this as reasonable, to her mother's relief; she had gotten enough rest to be more cheerful, even if it wasn't all she wanted. She checked and donned her outdoor gear with no more complaint, and even grinned with pride when her mother approved the check.

The way now led up Hemenway slope. The sun had set, though the sky was not yet completely dark. A few bright stars could be seen between slowly drifting clouds. They were still travelling very slowly as Kahvi continued to feel her way. Danna was walking now, but had been warned to stay behind her mother; with the memory of the glass still fresh and its pain still in her body, the child was quite willing to obey.

Kahvi knew of an air lock on this side of Hemenway, and was making their way toward it. She had decided that there was a good chance of Earrin's being inside the city. There would have been no chance for him to get back to the raft, and no evidence that he had tried. He had either stayed free and gone to a jail or the city for air, or been recaptured and brought to Hemenway as had apparently been the original Hiller intention.

In the old days, the citizens of Great Blue Hill had very seldom gone outdoors after dark. This seemed to have changed now, and she didn't dare approach the lock as casually as she might have done earlier. Since she had to travel so slowly anyway, the extra care wasn't as much nuisance as it might have been.

Once in sight of the lock pool, in fact, she decided to wait for a time to see whether any of these young people who seemed to go out a lot at night might be around, so she settled down in the center of a clump of bushes which provided materials for a hastily-made nest. Danna made no objection to going to sleep; there was nothing which interested her in the surrounding darkness.

Kahvi, in spite of her intention to keep watch, might have followed her daughter's example, but they had been there only a few minutes when sounds came from the nearby air lock. The moon was not up yet, but part of the pool reflected starlit sky, and the reflection was now broken by ripples and by dimly silhouetted human figures rising from the water. They were not showing any particular caution; there was an occasional splash, and some of them were talking. There was nothing in Kahvi's large collection of highly virtuous hangups which prohibited listening; information, including information on what other people were doing and planned to do, was necessary for life. She listened:

"D'you suppose it's gotten away yet?"

"Of course not. Les was watching; he'd have come to tell us if it had started anything he couldn't take care of himself, or if it had gotten loose before he could stop it. Besides, what could it do? It only tried the things we expected."

"And what," asked a female voice, "gives you the idea that it couldn't think of things we haven't? Of course it tried the obvious ones first. Sometimes they work. Remember how those two got away inside—and we still don't know where the other one is, you know."

"Of course not. It got over into the main city, where we can't look for it without getting the old fogies excited. Come on; we're getting this one. Maev thinks that it'll have used up all its ways of escape by now, and if it's still there we might as well bring it in for other tests. Make sure your sandals are tight, and go slowly; there's a lot of slime down that way, and travelling in the dark can put hard heads against harder rocks if you aren't careful. We'd better link up—who has the rope?"

Kahvi heard all this and drew the obvious conclusions. The two captives who had escaped must be Bones and Earrin, and the native had been recaptured. For some reason she was being held outside—some sort of testing, it appeared. This group was to bring her back into the city. Could Kahvi forestall them? Which way were they going? How was Bones being held? If the Hillers were going to rope together, the route must be dangerous; could she find it by that fact? Could she get there, over slime, ahead of the Hillers?

Quick decision was standard. Kahvi got to her feet, drawing the child up with her and signalling for silence, and began to retreat carefully. She moved quietly, not because she feared being heard but so as to continue hearing what the others might be saying as she worked her way around the lock pool in search of a slippery area.

"What if it *has* gotten away?"

"Then good breathing to it, of course. Les will be able to tell what happened—unless it ate him."

"They don't eat people, idiot."

"Why not, if they eat each other?" This question went unanswered, since there were no biochemists in the group. The one who had asked it went on after a pause. "I don't like the idea of getting close to that thing. I think we've learned enough from it. If it's still there I'm for putting more spears through it—"

"Why should a lot be any more use than one?"

"Then cut the thing to pieces and make a fire with it—unless Maev wants to cut it up to see what's inside."

"That may be next. It's up to her, but we bring it in the way it is. Come on."

"No. Wait. Look, I'll go down carefully; you come slowly behind me. If we do need weapons, at least I can give some warning so you can get off the rope in time."

"All right, but don't be too slow or we'll have the moon in our eyes."

Kahvi had heard enough; the last sentence told her which way to go—not precisely, perhaps, but nearly enough, since the distance couldn't be very great. She headed east, with Danna hurrying behind. They would have to take their chances on glass and slime now; if these Hillers were planning to cut Bones up she would have to be gotten away or at the very least warned.

The voices from behind grew louder; the main body was gaining—what of the one who was coming ahead of them? How far ahead was Bones? Could Kahvi get there in time to do anything but watch? There was noise behind, nearer than the voices. There—a little to the right—was that a clearing?

It was, and suddenly she could see Bones' figure silhouetted against the slowly brightening eastern sky. It would have to be warning; she could not possibly get there long enough before the others to give physical help. She called out loudly to Bones, and almost instantly a human figure rose in her path.

XIV

History, Hazily

Earrin turned his back on the woman and headed back toward the sunlit area. The pseudo-Bones followed. The woman, jolted by the Nomad's choice of language and even more startled and shocked by his accusation, stared silently until the two were out of sight. For the moment her thinking processes, such as they were, were paralyzed. She did not, of course, believe the unthinkable charge; but it was almost equally hard to believe that a Nomad would lie, and she was even less equipped than Earrin in background information and basic attitude to imagine any third possibility.

Her mind retreated to a more basic fact which she *could* handle. A Nomad and one of the Animals were wandering in the city breathing air that didn't belong to them. They should be ejected, but she couldn't possibly do this herself. The nearest people would be the children taking care of the air plants, who could hardly be useful either—but there might be a teacher or two there, and if not at least a child could go for real help. She headed after the intruders.

There was no one in sight when Earrin and his friend emerged into the sunlight. The plant area was much larger than the one in Hemenway where the other Bones had been captured; it extended for hundreds of meters along a curving shelf on the southern face of Great Blue Hill. The plant trays which filled it were no larger or more closely spaced, of course; they had to be moved around, and people had to move around them. They were slightly different in design from those on the raft; while they had the usual bubble-top protection from infecting spores, seated in channels of water, these units produced oxygen more rapidly. The gas bubbled out around the edges; on the raft, the bubbles had to be opened frequently to let oxygen out and carbon dioxide in. Pseudo-Bones could see that these plants must be fed with solid carbonates, presumably brought from collectors scattered through the city; Earrin did not grasp their operation until the other had explained it. This took a little time, since the scientific vocabulary of the gesture language was somewhat limited.

Most of the plants in sight, however, were food

producers quite familiar to Earrin, who did not hesitate to remove one of the plastic tents and start eating. The Observer did the same, making a different selection and stowing away a much larger quantity in spite of its smaller size.

The woman had been watching from the entrance to the tunnel and was wildly indignant, but resisted the impulse to rush out and tear the fruit and meat from the thieves. Even the little one was probably stronger than she. Where were the regular attendants?

There was only one answer to that; the plant shelf extended well to the west. To keep out of sight of the intruders she would have to go back into the tunnels and take a roundabout way in that direction. Neither Earrin nor smaller-Bones had noticed her arrival, and they did not see her departure. They were wondering why so many of the plants in sight appeared to be poorly nourished, though none seemed actually infected. Earrin knew, of course, that the population of Great Blue Hill was below its planned figure, but could never have believed that the air units would have been allowed to get so badly out of balance with the demand.

Two hundred meters to the west, the elderly woman emerged onto the shelf from another tunnel and found herself fairly close to a group of air attendants. To her delight, two of them were adults, and she rushed up to these blurting out her story. Both of them knew her and were able to make sense out of her rapid speech; some of the children had more difficulty.

"Slow down, Genda," one of the teachers said

soothingly. "You're saying that there's a Nomad in the air center, and he has one of the outside animals with him? You needn't be so excited. If it's the Nomad I think it is, he'll pay for his air if he hasn't already, and the animals don't breathe."

"That's what he tried to tell me, but I don't believe it. How can anything live without breathing? Try it yourself!"

"Let's not go into that," the other teacher interjected. He knew the futility of trying to reason with Genda on any subject connected with air. "If the Nomad said it—"

"But this Nomad *lies*!" exclaimed the older woman. "He said he didn't know there was an animal following him, and then a few minutes later I saw him *talking* to it!"

"I don't see what that proves—did you say talking? To one of the—" the teacher, a tall woman of about twenty with hair short enough for outdoor work but no sign of acid stain on her skin, broke off her question and turned to her companion eagerly. "Mort, do you suppose—"

Genda cut in. "Yes, talking to it, like Doctor Doolittle. He said he didn't know the thing, when he must have trained it!"

Mort, rather to his own surprise, managed to silence her with a gesture. "Zham, do you suppose she's right? That a man can actually talk to those things? I've heard stories, of course—we all have—of Nomads associating with those things and getting them to be helpful. Like Genda, I've always supposed it must be training if there were any truth in the stories at all; but—talking? This could be important."

"Talking." Genda was positive, and indifferent as usual to the fact that the man's remark had not been directed to her. Neither teacher responded.

"It's hard to believe, but we'll have to find out," Zhamia conceded. "Where are they, Gen?" The excited woman pointed. "All right, let's go see."

"And get them out of here?" asked Genda eagerly.

"Eventually. We'll have to find out more, first. They might have something really important to tell us."

"We know all that's important. Have you been listening to those Hemenway delinquents?"

"Don't be insulting. Of course not. But think, Gen—those youngsters are preaching that man and his way of life didn't destroy the world's air; they claim these creatures did. You know that."

"I pay no attention to the stupid children. They refuse to listen to—"

"But think, Gen. If someone can talk to these— these animals, we could find out the truth!"

"We know the truth."

"All right, but if these creatures can tell us that they didn't have anything to do with the change, and actually supply evidence that would make the Hemenway crowd see they were wrong and have to admit it, just think how it will quiet them down. Don't worry—we'll get payment from the Nomad for the air he's using if he hasn't paid already. Do you want to come and listen?"

"Yes!" exclaimed half a dozen children's voices at once.

"I meant Gen," Mort grinned, "but you young ones can certainly come if your trays are all right.

Keep your brains open—there are a lot more facts of life than air plants."

Earrin and his companion were not exactly surprised to see the group approaching them, but were very uncertain what to do about it. Their experience with the Hemenway group had seriously undermined their earlier beliefs about the non-violent nature of human beings in general and Hillers in particular, and the man's belief that Bones had been subjected to some mysterious treatment to reduce his bulk by nearly ninety percent was disquieting. Such an action had to be scientific in nature in spite of the Hill religion, and while Earrin was not nearly as religious as a typical city-dweller he had a very low opinion of hypocrisy. For one thing, it implied unpredictability, one of the least acceptable of human qualities from the Nomad viewpoint. What would this Hiller crowd do?

Its members didn't look particularly menacing, especially the children. If facial expressions could be trusted, their chief motive was curiosity. Even the two new adults showed no sign of the indignation and resentment so clearly displayed by the other woman; they, too, seemed curious. Their first words were both friendly and courteous.

"I'm Zhamia McDermott, this is Mort Dremm. You've met Genda, I understand, but she didn't give us your name."

"She never asked for it," Earrin replied. "I'm Earrin Fyn. I delivered some material you asked for a day or so ago, and am waiting for my pay and, I hope, more orders. This is Bones."

The Hillers were clearly excited.

"He has a name? He's really a person?" asked Mort. "We've heard stories, but never knew—we thought they were just—"

"Is Bones he or she?" asked Zhamia rather pointedly.

"I've never known," Earrin admitted. "My wife always refers to him as *she*. We've never been able to find out from him. He doesn't answer questions about that; acts as though he didn't understand them."

"But you can talk to—her?"

"Yes. He can hear, but not very well, and can't make sounds at all; doesn't have a voice. We've worked out a pretty good signal system over the years; I *think* we understand each other pretty well most of the time."

"Why Bones?" asked Mort. "Is it his real name that he told you, or one you gave him?"

"How could she have told them, with no voice?" asked Zhamia. Dremm blushed.

"It was my wife's idea," Earrin admitted. "As far as we can tell, he doesn't have any. Certainly not in the fins or tentacles, and we've seen the rest of his body squeeze into pretty strange shapes. It's hard to believe there's anything solid inside."

Neither of the teachers quite grasped this sort of humor, but both were too polite to ask for further explanation. Neither really had a chance, as Genda cut in angrily.

"He's a liar. I told you how I know."

Mort explained the older woman's reasoning as she had given it to the teachers. Earrin explained, keeping his own feelings under better control.

"The last time I saw Bones, he was the best part of a meter taller than I am. When I first saw him today I thought it was someone else—another of his people I'd heard was being kept a prisoner here. I didn't know it was really Bones until *he* recognized *me* and began talking to me in our own sign language."

"Couldn't your real Bones have met this one earlier and taught him—her—the language?"

"And to recognize me on sight? I last saw the real one only a day or so ago, and he'd been with us all the time for months before that. If there's been a smaller one around watching us and taking language lessons, neither Kahvi nor I saw it. No, this has to be the real Bones. He's shrunk. I found him just a little while ago in this city. The Hillers who captured me admitted they were keeping another of Bones' people for *experiments*, though they dodged that exact word. That's certainly what they were doing. They claimed that Bones' people came from another world, and had destroyed Earth's air; they want to change the air back, and think they have to kill the natives first so they won't interfere. They're using the ones they capture to find out how they can kill them. I don't know what they did to Bones, but it was certainly something which explains why people decided science was evil."

"*Is* evil!" snapped Genda. Earrin paid no attention.

"I'm sorry if I insulted this Genda person by saying she was involved in science, but she called me a liar, and *someone* here in this city of yours certainly is. When I told Genda I'd never seen this native before, I believed it. I'm willing to admit she's not the hypocrite, but don't try to tell me there aren't some around!"

"It's those Hemenway devils!" exclaimed Genda. "I might have known it! They're not just talking evil—denying the truth and the law—they're practising it as well. They're using *science*—they're *experimenting*!" Even in her rage, she had trouble uttering the forbidden words, and flushed in embarrassment as she did so. "They'll make the world even harder to live in unless they're stopped—we won't even have cities! I'm sorry I thought you were a liar, Earrin; I didn't want to believe it. You can see how I'd make the mistake. It's still hard to believe that—that civilized people—even those young ones—could—could—" She couldn't make herself use the words again.

Fyn accepted the apology, though he was really unable to care very much what this woman thought. The information about the social changes going on in Great Blue Hill was more interesting, and quite disturbing; if one could no longer be sure what these people were going to do, and especially if one could no longer be sure of close connection between what they promised and what they would do, he and Kahvi would have to reconsider very carefully their own future relations with the city and its people. If one could not regard the people as a unit, the planning would have to be much more complex. This was as new a problem to Fyn as it was to Bones.

It must have been the Hemenway group whose members had wanted the glass and copper, and he had no right to be using the air and food of the main city—or did that belong to all the inhabitants? And if some of them wanted the cargo and others didn't, who paid him from common property? It was too much for Earrin, and for the first time he became really worried about whether he and Kahvi would receive any return for their efforts. They could live without it of course; fundamentally they were completely independent of other people.

But man is a social animal.

He brought his attention back to the present; Zhamia was saying something.

"When Genda told us you were talking to Bones, it occurred to us we might get information which would force the delinquents to change their preaching," she said. "We might even get them to see their errors. No one knows how long the—pardon the term—animals have been around, but perhaps they have some idea of what really happened to the world's air. Most of us, of course, believe that sinners experimenting with pseudo-life made the change—they wanted nitrates to make food with, though I can't see what way that would work, and produced an organism which could take nitrogen from the air and release nitrates into the ground. It needed oxygen from the air, too, and worked too well. The Hemenway youngsters insist that the animals, which they call Invaders, did the same thing to get rid of the

oxygen so they could live here. I don't know how
they're explaining to themselves why Bones
doesn't seem to be bothered by the oxygen here in
the city, but I'm sure they have an answer. I wonder if Bones knows what really happened, though;
have you ever asked?

"No. Neither of us ever thought of it," Earrin
admitted.

"Will you?"

"Sure. I've never really believed there was
enough oxygen loose in the air to make it breathable, but it would be nice to find out." He ignored
Genda's gasp of outrage and turned to the Observer.

The children listened and watched in fascina-
tion. Since the man's gestures served mainly to
supplement his words, helping Bones distinguish
phonemes which Observer auditory and nervous
systems could not distinguish, some of the more
observant youngsters began to catch on to the
system very quickly. The return signals, however,
were another matter; they were made not only
with the two main handling tentacles but with the
dozen much finer tendrils which formed a fore-
and-aft fringe across the top of the head on each
side of the great mouth. Since the translation
came at intervals rather than continuously, none
of the children made any progress with this aspect
of the system.

The translation itself was not always clear;
neither Fyn nor the human listeners had an
adequate information background. Human beings in general still knew some physics and as-

tronomy, since many books still existed. They
knew much more chemistry, since the technology
which kept the remnants of humanity alive was
based on biochemical products of earlier times.
Mankind was in more or less the position of a
motorcycle gang whose members could not have
built their machines from metal ores or refined
their own fuel, but were kept supplied with spare
parts and gasoline. The continuation of the
supplies was due to the fact that the resources of
the biochemical culture were self-renewing—
pseudoliving organisms and tissues. No person
now living could have produced the pseudolife
from raw chemicals, but many of them could still
manipulate it with the aid of such agents as the
Evolution plant's enzymes.

With this sort of limitation on human knowledge, it was impossible for all of Bones' account
to be completely clear even to the adults. Fyn's
translation of Bones' pronouns was also very
foggy. The Observer had no conception whatever
of the difference between "he" and "she," as Earrin already knew. What affected the present attempt at communication was the fact that the
native also lacked any real grasp of the difference
between "I" and "we," and understood "you"
only because of long association with the raft family. Earrin's translation was therefore much more
of a paraphrase than a direct quote.

It was clear that Bones had arrived on Earth
after the air change, and was not responsible for
it. He/they had travelled frozen in a body which an
astronomer of earlier times would unhesitatingly

have called a comet nucleus. These, travelling slowly between the stars, were constantly carrying vast numbers of Bones' species through the Galaxy in obedience to their basic psychological drive—the need to *know*. Automatic controls would place the comet into an appropriately close orbit and awaken the crew when and only when sensing apparatus identified an atmosphere as being primarily nitrogen, with enough traces of oxides of that element to indicate the presence of nitro-life. Bones' vehicle was the comet which now rode sixty degrees behind the moon in the latter's orbit; his/their landing craft was on the sea bottom thousands of kilometers from the Boston area.

The fact that all this came as though it were a personal memory confused Fyn, and did not get through his translation very well. The other human beings were therefore even less clear about the matter. There was no doubt, however, that Bones was denying categorically that his kind had had anything to do with the change in the world's air.

Zhamia, who had the best conception of the times and distances which must be involved, was rather suspicious of the account. She admitted that it was hard for her to believe in a coincidence which had apparently brought Bones' comet to the Solar system within a few years, or at most a few centuries, of the time the change had taken place. She put this to the Observer.

Bones made it clear that no coincidence was involved. Many comets had undoubtedly visited the System; until the Earth conditions were correct, they would merely have gone into short-period orbits around the sun and waited, boiling off some of their ice at each perihelion passage until they were consumed. Their personnel would have died without ever being aroused. When one crew was awakened, the other comets would, if they possessed mass enough, leave automatically in search of another habitable system.

Fyn could not see how the crews could face such a fate, and said so. It was Bones' attempt to explain why they didn't mind which started the man toward the realization that the being now talking was not, in fact, "his" Bones. There was no clear communication here; the Observers had no grasp of the concept of individual death, and Fyn's difficulty had not been understood at all. From the answer, the man at first got the idea that Bones was immortal. This was in a sense, as far as personality was concerned, true; it was of course very wrong in detail. The "units" could and did, eventually, die.

Genda had listened, though all she really noticed was the statement that the Observers had arrived after the change in Earth's atmosphere. This supported her view of orthodoxy, and she made no secret of her delight.

"That will let those delinquents know the poor animals aren't to blame for anything! Let's go over the Hemenway and tell them right now!" She was actually smiling. The other three adults looked at each other silently; two or three of the children giggled until Zhamia caught their eyes. The teacher spoke gently.

"How will we make them believe it, Gen?" she asked. "We don't really have proof—just Bones' story. Would you have believed it if we'd been told his people *had* made the air change?"

"But he didn't!" The implications of Zhamia's question were simply beyond the older woman. "He told the truth, as much of it as he knew. It was sin that caused the change—you know what kind of sin. Nothing else could have changed the whole world so much."

Earrin translated this to Bones, not because he felt that Genda's opinions carried much weight but because he assumed that any knowledge which would help predict the behavior of a Hiller might be as useful to the Observer as to Earrin himself. The answer was surprising, and for some seconds after it was translated it silenced even Genda.

"It may be the action of your kind which changed your world; I have been trying to decide. However, I must also decide why it always seems to happen, on every world I have seen."

XV

Debate, Directed

"Every one?" Mort took the question up instantly. "How many worlds are there? Have you visited them all?" The idea that Bones was immortal had also dawned on the teacher. He watched Fyn eagerly as the question was translated.

"I certainly have not visited them all; how many there may be is knowledge not yet acquired. I have landed only on those with proper living conditions, and presumably only a small fraction of those. I can remember only sixteen, directly, but many units have made—" there was a pause, as even Bones had to grope for a meaningful

signal—"Branch trips. Doubtless some, perhaps
many, of these have also found habitable worlds,
but the units have not rejoined with their
memories. Knowledge itself grows dim with time,
but I am quite certain of the sixteen I mentioned.
On every one of them there was much chemical
evidence that some time earlier—always until
now very much earlier—the world had had an
oxygen-rich atmosphere. I have been trying to
learn why this always changed, and it was a delight to find a world where the change seems to
have been so recent. Perhaps I can really know.
Perhaps your companion is right."

Genda was too delighted even to be angry at the
"perhaps."

"Have any oxygen-breathing people ever been
living on the worlds you have seen?" asked
Zhamia.

"No, this is the first. This is why I am hopeful.
Perhaps some of your people can supply
knowledge—I have never before learned things
indirectly, from other beings. This itself is a fascinating new field in which to learn. Had it not
been so, I would have tried to escape much earlier.
There was little I learned during the months I was
a captive, but there was that great hope."

This statement, of course, distracted Earrin
from his interpreting job.

"Months? But you've been in their hands only a
day or so!" The true situation had been filtering
slowly into Fyn's mind, but had not quite reached
conscious level. Bones' earlier story had started
the flow; the latest statement cracked the dam.

"No. I had no way to judge the time precisely, until the other unit arrived; but this unit now knows where the moon and planets are in the sky. It was in the cell for eight of the moon's orbits, plus five days."

The dam was broken, but common sense fought the flood valiantly.

"That's impossible! Less than two days ago you were helping pull our raft across Boston Harbor."

"Yes, of course. What is impossible about that?"

"You can't be in two different places at the same time, doing two different things!"

"I think we are having more trouble with your communication code. Remember, the two units met long enough to exchange memories while both were captive."

"I don't understand."

"Neither do we," Mort cut in. "Could you tell us what's going on, Fyn? You haven't been translating."

"Can't. I'm too mixed up myself. Wait until I can get this straight, please." The Nomad had continued to keep his eyes on Bones' gestures.

"We were able to use the *real* speech." The Observer tried to use less direct terminology, though the gesture language provided little wherewithal. "You know—at least—I thought—you and Kahvi sometimes—but perhaps I was wrong. Tell me, is the sound system really your only way of transferring information—memories—knowledge—from one of your kind to another?"

"There's writing."

"But that is just an even less direct use of your sound code. There is nothing *more* direct?"

"No."

The Observer stood motionless, except for eyeballs which shifted slowly from one of the human beings to another, for fully two or three minutes.

Fyn was equally bemused. Common sense had stopped fighting back. He had just about grasped the true situation with the natives—he and Kahvi would always think of them as plural, and as native, since they could live on Earth unprotected. The facts that he had been wrong about the "experimenting" and that the small Bones facing him was not, in body, the Bones he and his wife had known for years, were just about at the accepted-knowledge status.

At last he brought the teachers and children up to date on the communication. They were fascinated. Genda heard, but was dissatisfied; she had been counting on some assurance, somewhere within the story, that Science had indeed destroyed the world's air. The Observer's claim that this might be the case but he didn't really know irritated her almost as much as Earrin's unwillingness to take her word for it; after all, she *did* know. Earrin and the teachers were rather angry with Genda, but Bones was fascinated. Psychology was another totally new field to a mind which had not only never met another intelligent species until now, but had never encountered a different mind in its own. This crowd of *individuals*, cut off from each other except through crude and time-consuming code symbols, was a revelation—a brand new field of knowledge—indeed, a whole set of such fields. It was obvious that the incomplete and distorted picture of the universe transmitted by words would have fantastically unpredictable effects on those minds; the code symbols themselves would probably take the place of the reality they were supposed to transmit much of the time. Genda was a most fascinating example.

It would not occur to Bones for a long time that the Observer's sensory impressions were just as much a coded representation of reality as were human words. So were the molecular patterns which recorded those impressions, and passed them from one Observer unit to another. The species was a good scientist, but not yet a philosopher.

Genda was finally persuaded to settle, for the time, for Bones' concession that her belief was possible; it was one of those things which a scientist could not call *knowledge*. All the human listeners except Genda could see this viewpoint easily enough. Such terms as *UFO* and *Chariot of the Gods* had not survived. Common sense had, of necessity, though the teachers might have been bothered if anyone had called their attitude scientific. They were, in their own way, as religious as Genda, though far less bigoted.

With the collective nature of Bones' mind now fairly clear, the question of what had happened to the "other" Bones had to be faced. Events up to the time the two units had shared memories through the bars were clear enough. The smaller unit had managed to escape observation by descending several levels at the first opportunity after their separation. This had been a matter of luck, since there had been no knowledge of the Hill's population arrangement to provide guidance. Hours of unguided wandering had been ended by a decision to go up for food, based on the same logic which had guided Earrin. The Nomad had been found first. Where the original Bones might be was a matter of guesswork; the teachers had heard nothing of even one Observer wandering about the Hill, much less of two. The best guess seemed to be that Bones-One was still in the Hemenway area, free or otherwise.

Earrin, however, was starting to develop another worry. While he had no real reason to suppose that his family were anywhere but on the home raft, he knew that he should get back there himself before long. Otherwise, his wife would take some sort of action. He didn't know what it would be, and certainly felt more trust in her general competence than in his own, but did not want to return to find them missing. It might be possible, of course, to guess what she would be doing and even what she was expecting him to do—they had, after all, been together for a number of years—but Earrin would feel much better and less undecided if he managed to get home before she yielded to the urge for action.

The Nomad was therefore more pleased than offended when Genda began resuming her hints about intruders who used up city air. He said nothing about being owed air or anything else.

The teachers, however, reacted differently, and even the children looked embarrassed.

"Genda!" exclaimed Zhamia. "You can't want these people to go. It's the first real chance we've had to learn—"

"We don't need to learn some things!"

Even Earrin could see that the old woman's personality was crystallized, but Mort felt bound to keep on trying.

"That may be so, Gen," he said quietly, "but don't you want to teach? I've heard you complain so much about the people who don't have your firmness—not just the Hemenway kids and their heresy, but people like Zhamia and me who are a bit weak on details. You know people get tired of listening to the old words, but maybe Bones and Earrin can provide new ones which will help convince them."

A more objective mind than Genda's would have caught the weakness in this argument—the obvious possibility that new information was as likely to undermine the faith as to support it. However, she was quite unable to entertain the idea that she might be wrong, so this risk never occurred to her. Earrin was tempted to point it out to her, so that she would not be persuaded to let the strangers stay. Then it occurred to him that he didn't have to stay anyway, so he kept quiet.

Of course, if Zhamia and Mort wanted him and Bones to provide still more information, perhaps they should stay and do so; the chance of getting on really good terms with the Hillers would be too good to miss. Even Earrin, with fourteen years of

Nomad life behind him and a complete confidence in his own ability to take care of life's problems, was willing to accept increased security for himself and even more for his family. Kahvi's first baby, and her last two, had lived only a few weeks; Fyn was ready to go a long way to improve the chances for the next one.

He did not hear Genda's reply to the teacher's argument; he was too deeply immersed in his own thinking. He should get back to the raft soon. He should maintain friendly contact with Mort and Zhamia. He should get Bones-One out of the hands of the Hemenway delinquents, if Bones didn't solve that problem by himself. It took him some time to resolve these conflicting needs—typically, as his wife would have said with a smile and Earrin himself easily admitted. Just as typically, when the plan did develop he put it into execution with no further thought. This was at least excusable in an adult Nomad; such a person had to have the right answers on file. When problems did arise, there was very seldom much time to solve them.

"Are all these people you dislike—the Hemenway ones—oxygen junkies, Genda?" he asked. "The jail where I landed and where several of them met me has waster's air in it. I only met one person inside, but something the others said made me think he was part of their group."

"I didn't know they were *that* bad," sniffed the purist, "but it doesn't surprise me much." The reaction of the teachers was much more constructive, and Earrin congratulated himself silently.

"Mort! We can't leave a safety building in that condition! And if the young people have been responsible for their upkeep, maybe a lot of them— or all of them—we'll have to get some nitro culture. Earrin can—"

"Earrin *can*," Mort cut in, "but we can't ask him to. In the first place, he has his own home to take care of. In the second, if these youngsters are all O-junkies we'll need a lot more people to fix things over their objections anyway. If Earrin wants to help for reasonable pay, that's one thing; but it's a city job."

A child's voice cut in. The youngsters had been listening with an attention and silence which might have been startling a couple of millennia before, but which the adults present all took for granted. Even in the cities, people walked so nearly hand-in-hand with death that discipline was one of the first necessities learned. This was the chief reason why Mort and Zhamia were so concerned at the news that the Hemenway youngsters might be oxygen-wasters as well as heretics.

"You've been talking about practical lessons," the child said, "for a long time now. Would this be a good time for them?" The teachers looked a little startled for a moment.

"It certainly would," Zhamia admitted, "but we could take only Betty outside. We'll have to get the parents of you others. We can't leave the air room here unattended, either. Let's see. We'll pick half of you by whack, and those can go and get their parents. We'll meet at North-Up-Two. The rest of you will have to stay on duty here. Mort, do you have the gold?"

"Sure." The man drew an old medal from his harness pouch. "I'm ready." He turned his back on the others. "Face goes, inscription stays. Pick one." Zhamia touched one of the children.

"Toss," she said quietly.

The ceremony took only a few minutes. Seven "goes" were tossed before everyone had been touched, but there were no complaints; all were used to the method.

"I'm coming, too," Genda said abruptly. The others merely nodded; regardless of their preferences, she had the right to come if she pleased.

However, it was nearly two hours before the group was outside. Most of the time was spent in a large room with a huge map of the Blue Hills area which Earrin and Bones did their best to memorize, while assignments to the various jails and agreements on where and when to meet were made.

Once through the lock, most of the family groups went off in different directions toward their assigned buildings. All were carrying supplies of the appropriate spores or pseudolife fragments. The teachers, their ten-year-old Betty, Genda, Earrin, and Bones-Two started the three kilometer trip northward toward the raft. It was fairly late afternoon, but they hoped to reach it before dark. Genda walked silently, but kept her eyes roving over everything they passed. The child asked almost constant questions which were answered usually by her parents but sometimes passed on to Earrin or even Bones. The Nomad said nothing except when answering or interpreting; he was learning quite enough without steering the conversation.

Genda suddenly stopped and pointed. "Look!," she snapped. "Those young creatures have been making new life forms, too."

Earrin was curious. "That's just a Newell block," he said. "They've been around for years. You folks are always making variations; what's wrong with that? I've bought lots of new kinds of food and air plants from you Hillers over the years."

"Taking advantage of natural changes is one thing. Making something entirely new involves the Evil."

"But what's new about this? It's grown for years—since long before I was born—around some of the cities. My raft is made of it. I sold a piece to you people three or four years ago for a very nice milk plant. I don't know why this one is growing here; it may have been planted on purpose, or someone accidentally dropped a piece. It's been here for several years, certainly—it's big enough almost to make another raft."

"You mean it's natural?" Genda was unconvinced.

"I don't know, but I doubt it. It seems to have no natural enemies, and almost completely stops growing when it reaches about four cubic meters. Pseudolife was planned that way to minimize the risk of its spreading out of control, you know. You haven't been outdoors much, have you? I know there are other samples of this stuff growing around."

"I haven't seen any," was the rather evasive reply. Fyn didn't press the question; Zhamia and her daughter looked at each other and barely managed to conceal their smiles.

They were now on the south slope of the last hill which barred their sight of the raft, and when they topped it Fyn was relieved to see that his home was still there. He was less happy to see a dozen people busy around the site where the cargo had been left. Just shoreward of this point was something which had not been there before. It was a dome-shaped structure fully ten meters across and half as high.

Earrin had of course never seen an igloo, so the resemblance escaped him. He was not yet close enough to see the panes of glass among the spongy block of Newell tissue, but two or three of these windows were so placed as to reflect sunlight toward the newcomers, so their nature could be guessed.

There was no way to be certain that the workers were members of the Hemenway group, but it seemed likely. Fyn, after a moment's thought, turned to Bones.

"Get into the water before these people see you, and wait at the raft. If Kahvi or Danna are there, tell them what's happening. These are probably the same people who were interested in finding out how to kill you."

"They are. I recognize some of them," the Observer gestured. The slender form promptly made

its way back down the southeast side of the hill,
and slipped over to the water. The human beings
resumed their walk toward the jail.

They were not seen until they were almost at the
building; then one of the masked workers looked
up, and immediately called to the others. As had
been agreed, Zhamia and Genda went at once to
the air lock with their supplies of nitrogen-
producers, while Mort, Earrin, and Betty went on
toward the new structure. It was understood that
if anything even slightly suggestive of violence
were to start, the women and the child were to run
back toward the city at full speed, while the men
did what they could to delay pursuit. Neither of
the men actually believed that anything of the
sort could happen, but Bones had by now told of
the glass caltrops.

Earrin would have preferred to check with
Kahvi before talking to this group, but it seemed
unwise to head for the raft right now. Maybe she
would see him and come ashore to help.

And maybe she wouldn't. Behind the approaching Hillers, now close enough to recognize indi-
vidually, a short distance out in the water, the
figure of the smaller Bones suddenly appeared
and stood upright. It was close enough for even
Earrin to see clearly. There was only one likely
reason why the being had not stayed at the raft as
requested, and the message sent by the gesturing
tentacles was no surprise.

"There is no one on the raft."

The native promptly disappeared again.

XVI

Action, Antagonistic

Neither Kahvi nor Bones had made any plans
for such an event, but both acted as though there
had been careful rehearsal. The woman did not
even slow down, but hurtled with her full running
speed into the man who had suddenly appeared in
her path. This unfortunate had heard her voice as
she called to Bones, but had not seen her in time.
He was therefore not braced for any impact, and
went over backward. Even worse from his viewpoint, Kahvi had crossed her arms in front of her
body and taken the force on her elbows in an
almost instinctive gesture to protect the baby.

The man's ribs were not actually broken, but it was some days before he was sure of that.

His immediate trouble was landing in the glass-covered area, flat on his back. His howl warned the woman, and since the collision had almost stopped her anyway, she was able to keep her feet out of the caltrops.

Bones, fully aware of the location of the glass, made even better use of the incident; the body of the guard, writhing though it was, made an adequate bridge. It was too dark to signal to Kahvi, but communication was not needed. The woman snatched up Danna, Bones pulled the sandals from the feet of the guard, and they were off down and around the hill. Kahvi confessed afterward that she had been tempted to stay and trip some of the others into the glass, but admitted she was glad she hadn't. The shrieks of the single victim, fading as they fled, did not provide the anticipated pleasure. She felt sick again, but managed to keep it under control.

Neither she nor Bones could tell whether they were being pursued. Some, judging by the voices, had stayed to help the guard, but others might be following. It seemed unwise to wait to find out.

They paused briefly while Bones took over Danna and gave the sandals to the woman. She fastened them on after some difficulty, and they went on. Kahvi was leading the group around the hill toward the west; her first months as a Nomad had been passed mostly on that side of Great Blue Hill, and she was certain of finding a breathing refuge there. Her cartridges and Danna's still had many hours in them after their recent pause in another jail, but some Nomad decisions were reached without detailed thought. Her goal was the raft, but she would not head toward it without checking on possible pursuers; and she would not make that check without being close to a breathing refuge.

They were travelling slowly now, even with Bones carrying the main burden. Kahvi was not worrying about glass as long as her feet were protected, but she was tired and half way through a pregnancy; and the best of breathing masks interferes with activity.

They came finally to a jail on the northwest slope of Great Blue Hill, which suited the woman's purpose. Kahvi led the way to a thicket of realwood on the farther side of the structure, and all concealed themselves inside. Danna went to sleep in a hastily assembled nest, and Kahvi devoted some time to exchanging information with the Observer. While doing this, however, she looked frequently back along the way they had come.

Presently the moon was high enough to illuminate the landscape plainly, and drown out the faint light which had been visible through the roof of the jail. As it grew brighter, two figures appeared on the shoulder of the hill where the trio had travelled. They were walking slowly. Kahvi, with no tracking experience, did not guess at the reason; she assumed that they had followed by sound, and wondered why they had taken so long to arrive.

The pursuers saw the jail as soon as they reached the near slope. One pointed, and their speed increased. One of them waited a few meters from the air lock while the other quietly circled the building; then they approached the lock together, and one of them entered.

To Kahvi's surprise, conversation sounded from the building almost at once. It hadn't occurred to her that there might be someone already inside. The waiting pursuer also seemed a little taken aback, and after a few seconds of listening he, too, disappeared through the lock. Kahvi, uttering a quick "wait here" in words only, and hoping that Bones would understand, dashed to the near wall of the jail and was at the top in seconds. Eavesdropping had been useful before and was certainly worth trying again. As before, she was careful about moonlight and gold jewelry.

This place was better lighted inside. The two who had just entered were easily recognizable, since they were dripping wet. The three others appeared to form a family group; they were a man and woman somewhere near Kahvi's own age, and a boy of nine or ten. This was not too surprising; Kahvi knew that both custom and law in most cities worked toward a tight family knitting. Parents were expected to take active part in their children's education, and be with them whenever anything important or dangerous was due to happen. It was quite understandable that the parents would be outdoors if the child had to be.

It was much less obvious why the child had to be out, but Kahvi gave little thought to the matter; there was a much more interesting difference between the groups. The newcomers had promptly removed their masks, but the family, who had evidently been inside for some time, had theirs on. There was an obvious explanation; it really qualified only as an inference, but it seemed a very, very strong inference.

This jail must be oxygen-loaded, too. There must be a surprising number of oxygen-junkies in Great Blue Hill; what had been happening to the city since Kahvi had been Nomadded, anyway?

There was still more to be inferred. The family members were normal people, and they knew about the changed air. The conversation came as no surprise. One of the newcomers was speaking.

"How did you know about the oxygen? Don't tell me you could smell it!" The masked adults shook their heads negatively, and the man replied aloud.

"Of course not; but look at the trays. Every last one of them has Bence or Trendell growths—O-makers. There isn't a nitrogen maker or dilution tube in the place."

"You noticed that as soon as you got here?"

"Of course. Who could be sloppy enough not to make that check in a new building? I'm glad to say that Ray, here, was—" The other cut in.

"You weren't *expecting* something of the sort, were you? Why are you here so late at night?"

"Well," the father admitted reluctantly, "as a matter of fact, yes. We've checked several buildings. We—"

"Never mind softening it. You came to check the air, on purpose?"

"Yes."

"Why? And you say you've been to others?"

"Yes, several. It was reported that many of the safety buildings had been sabotaged by oxygen wasters, and a lot of families came out to make repairs."

Both newcomers stiffened, and the one who had hitherto been silent asked quickly, "You brought N-cultures with you?"

"Yes, of course."

"Have you spoiled any of the O-plants yet?"

"We've fixed them, yes, of course. It was the first thing we did. Of course it will take a while before the air becomes normal, so we're staying masked for the night."

The two looked at each other, frowning. One seemed uncertain; the other was more organized.

"Which ones did you—fix?"

The woman answered after a moment's hesitation, "We're not exactly sure—it didn't seem to make much difference, so we didn't pay a great deal of attention."

"You're a liar!" was the snarled answer. "With three of you doing it, you'd never have left it to chance who did what. You'd never have risked destroying them all!"

The husband straightened up indignantly. "Watch your language, waster. There was no danger of doing them all; our N-spores couldn't grow in a Bence culture. We probably did do all the others, if it's so important to you. We don't lie, and if you think anyone would on such a minor matter please get out of here—you'll be giving the boy dangerous ideas, though I'd trust him not to be much impressed by your kind!"

"Breathe it! Don't tell me you'd spoil all of even one of the cultures. Even if you're stupid enough to think that your masks will keep extra oxygen out, you can't be dumb enough to risk the last of any culture." He laughed at the expressions visible even with the masks in place. "Deep thinkers, aren't you? All a rebreather bellows does is mix the gas from your cartridge with some of the out-door air. You're like a couple of Nomads—follow the rules without any thinking!"

"Good for them!" retorted the woman. "At least, they know about rules. It was a Nomad who told us about the vandalism in the jails. I'd rather look like one of them than be mistaken for one of you if-a-little-is-good-more-is-better types. Now get out of the way. We're leaving."

The taller of the addicts was wearing an un-pleasant smile. "Sure. Two of you go any time you want. The kid stays until we know just which O-plants you heirs of righteousness ruined."

"You can't stop him. We'll—"

"You'll what? Even if you count him, the three of you aren't strong enough to get past us—*without having your masks ruined.* Think it over. Lots of spare cartridges here, but only a few masks, and we can take care of those before you can save them. It's *so* much easier to smash things than to fix them, isn't it?" Before either parent could move he had taken two long strides to the small boy, and seized the tubes running from cartridges to bellows. "Shall I pull?"

"No!" the mother almost shrieked.

For a moment, the watching Kahvi didn't know whether to be more indignant at the junky's threat or at the mother's lack of firmness. Then she imagined Danna in the boy's place and understood. Decision was a little more difficult than usual, but having decided, Kahvi's action was of course unhesitating.

"It won't do you any good!" she called, rising to her knees on the wall. "There'll be plenty of others along tomorrow. You junkies may as well let them all out, and enjoy what you can of your oxygen. If it takes the others long enough to get here, maybe you'll be able to see which of your plants got fixed. But leave that boy alone, or we'll come in there now and make you sorry. Bones! Danna! Come over here and cover this air lock!"

The people in the jail looked up in astonishment at Kahvi's figure, clearly visible in the moonlight. The addicts, startled, did nothing else; the parents seized their son and plunged into the lock pool. They emerged outside just as Bones arrived with Danna, and at the sight of the Observer and its burden they froze almost as completely as the two still within. Kahvi's voice restored them.

"All right, don't worry about Bones. She's working with me, and I trust her with my daughter.

Leave your boy outside, and come back in with Bones and me. There's work to do." She shifted to sign language, letting Bones know her plans, and the native set Danna down beside the other child. Kahvi descended, a little awkwardly, from the wall and led the way to the lock. Bones followed immediately, the other pair farther back and more hesitant. By the time they were inside, most of the action had finished.

Bones, at a gesture from the woman, had seized the two men, holding their arms at their sides with ropy tentacles. Kahvi was busy scooping up masks and cartridges. She gestured to the others to do the same, as they wiped water from their mask windows.

"We'll leave a few cartridges, of course, but be sure to get all the masks—no, we'll leave one," the Nomad said briskly. "If something happens to the roof they can stay alive by sharing it, but won't be able to get into mischief. You two—" she addressed the prisoners—"can play around with the cultures all you want, but I'd suggest you be very disciplined. If you spoil any more oxygen, you might just have to get to the next jail holding your breaths by turns. As I remember, it's about five hundred meters a little south of west, over two hills. Use your judgment, if overloading yourselves with oxygen has left you any."

One of the addicts answered. "Very nice, Nomad. We know how pure and righteous you all are, and of course you have every right to force other people to go along with your morals. You must feel really virtuous, going around with an Invader. I suppose you'll help it destroy the cities the way they did the rest of the world—*you* won't be bothered, will you?"

"No time for mythology just now," Kahvi replied briefly. "If you feel the need for straight oxy, at least you could build your own gas-houses. These buildings were made to save lives, and I haven't any time to waste on free-loaders. Got everything, you two? All right, Bones—" she shifted her burden to one arm and gestured with the other—"hold them until we're outside with the children. Then do anything you can think of to keep them from interfering with you, and come along. We'll head for the raft; we have plenty of air." She started down the air lock steps, then turned back. "One more thing, now that I think of it. These other folks are barefoot, I notice. I'll take your sandals. I don't like those nasty bits of glass you oxy-lovers have invented."

The verb stung the prisoners, not yet entirely free of their upbringing. "We didn't invent them. They showed up in a pseudolife mutation that used to make fiberglass for insulation, so we used them. Anyone would have."

Kahvi, adding the sandals to her burden, sniffed audibly through her mask. "Anyone not burdened by ethics or conscience might. Knowing that I've picked several dozen of the things out of my child, though, you'll excuse me for excluding such 'people' from the human species, I'm sure. Free breathing."

She disappeared into the pool. Bones gave her about five seconds than, tossed the prisoners against the far wall and lunged through before they recovered their footing.

Outside, Kahvi had introduced herself and Danna to the others, and learned their names. The woman was Viah Renuchi, her husband Jonathan Demang, and their son Ray Vellik. They had never met Nomads before, nor had they seen one of Bones' kind, but of course had heard of both. They had the usual city tendency to regard Kahvi as a rather low variety of human being, but the fact that she could converse with Bones forced them to modify their views about both. They were a little awed by the Observer.

"I have to get back to our raft with Danna and learn what Earrin's doing," Kahvi explained when introductions were complete. "He must have been in the city. You said that a Nomad brought the word about oxygen in the jails, and we're the only ones I know of around here. You didn't see him?"

"I guess we did," replied Jonathan. "He was with the people who did the briefing, and they referred to him a lot, but never by name. He was about your height, a little lighter in build, blue eyes, rather narrow face, and had a much smaller one of these creatures with him."

"That's Earrin. There was another native in the city and Bones here did meet her or him or it, but neither had met Earrin at that time. The two escaped together from some of your oxy-wasters;

Bones was recaptured but brought outside, where I found her a little while ago. The other one must have found Earrin, or been found by him. If they were with your people, they must have gone back to the raft, or at least be on the way. I must get back too, and get into step with him and the other native. Do you want to come too, or go back to the city? There's plenty of air at the raft, and you'll find out more about what these young people of yours are doing. It looks as though more of you ought to find out; or would you rather get Ray back indoors before you do anything else?"

"He's all right as long as he's with us," Viah replied. "We never have done much outdoors, but he needs the training, and would probably get it better with you around. Besides, we're book copiers, and maybe you could help us find better writing tissue or ink. We've heard that Nomads sell things like that."

"Maybe," agreed Kahvi. "All right, come along. It's about three kilometers on the map, so I suppose between four and five walking. We can travel all right by moonlight. I hope we don't need the sandals; if we run into glass we'll have to carry the kids, and I don't know what we'll do with Bones. You wear sandals, and I'll go ahead barefoot so the young ones won't be first to run into it."

The others knew nothing of the glass caltrops, and were suitably horrified by Kahvi's account. They had barely heard of the Hemenway delinquents, and couldn't guess what was going on—the news industry was one of the casualties of the change. They were still, however, willing to risk the trip to the shore. Kahvi, hoping fervently that she was right in believing that the glass had been sown only in special areas for special purposes, led the way.

XVII

Mail, Melanic

The message was no real surprise to Earrin, but it did not make him at all happy. He was not yet very worried about his family, but it would be nice to know whether Kahvi had gone somewhere on her own initiative or had been persuaded as he himself had been some twenty-four hours before. It didn't seem a good idea to ask those approaching, though it didn't occur to him that they would lie. He noticed the footgear they were wearing, but it meant nothing to him; he had not had Kahvi's experience, and the smaller Bones had not included the glass detail in their conversations.

Fyn was spared the need of deciding what to say; one of the approaching Hillers opened the conversation. The Nomad had not recognized him, but evidently they had met.

"I'm sorry you chose not to stay with us, Fyn. I think if you'd listened you'd have understood why we wanted you."

Earrin raised his eyebrows, though his mask hid the gesture. "It seemed to me I did know," he replied. "You weren't too happy about my use of the word, as I recall, but you wanted me to help you capture a friend of mine for experimental use."

There was no sharp reaction to the scientific word this time, but there was little friendliness in the voice.

"I see you've met up with Genda, the World's major mouth. Been getting your faith renewed?"

"Not exactly. Some of us Nomads listen critically to people—not everyone really knows what he's talking about, you realize."

"And naturally, if they don't know, you don't listen." The sarcasm was obvious.

"When people waste oxygen on purpose I don't need Genda or anyone else to tell me their judgment needs polishing," the Nomad said quietly. "Look, friend, I didn't come to argue. If you'll give me the plants we agreed on as payment for the metal and glass I see you've been using, I'll listen to anything you want, but most happily to an order for more material. You can straighten out anything else with Genda, or Mort here, or anyone and everyone else in the city. You can all go on straight oxygen as far as I care. I'd be happier, of course, if you'd leave the jail here usable as a breathing place when we make deliveries. We don't absolutely need it, but we always feel happier when a spare is in reach, and our own nearest one is several kilos away. We'll put up with this situation if we have to, but the offense to our feeling about waste may cost you more on future deals."

"And if we don't want to make any future deals?" asked a woman.

"We'll live with that. There are other cities."

The woman pulled in her horns. "I suppose we could leave old-style air in one building, especially since we have another almost ready right beside it. Your glass was very useful, and I suppose Genda and that other woman are spoiling the air in the jail anyway. We do find you useful, I admit—more than we realized originally. You do know about the Invader that was following you, don't you?"

"Yes, but as you know I don't call him an Invader. He's a friend of mine, and has been for some years. I'll be glad to tell you all I know about him, but I won't help you experiment on how to kill him. He says he didn't have anything to do with the world's air change, and I believe him."

"Why believe him rather than us?" These Hillers seemed neither surprised nor excited at the revelation that the "Invaders" were intelligent enough to talk. It was, after all, consistent with their basic dogma. "I know you Nomads will believe anyone, but can't you see that if those things *had* destroyed the world's air, they'd certainly deny it?"

"No, I can't. The reason I believe Bones rather than you wasters lies in what you just said—*you* believe there are reasons for lying. That, as far as I'm concerned, says all I need to know about you."

The Hiller was silent. Mort and Zhamia, who had been brought up with the respect for truth necessary for any reasonably large society but who lacked the Nomads' extreme attitude, were amused at the oxygen-waster's discomfiture. Their daughter was greatly impressed, looking at Earrin with admiration but saying nothing.

Another of the sandal-wearing group took up the debate.

"We don't say lying is good," she pointed out, "but you can't blame us for realizing that there are people—and things—who don't always tell the truth. We can admire idealism, but we've found the need to be a little realistic ourselves."

"So you believe what you've decided to believe." Fyn was plainly sarcastic, too.

"We don't know what to believe, but the Invader idea fits what facts we have and seems reasonable. We are willing to have more information—"

"You mean it's a hypothesis and you need more data, though you didn't like to admit that earlier," Earrin said rather brutally. Mort and his wife were properly shocked; their daughter felt the pleasurable thrill which a child of an earlier millennium would have gotten from hearing an adult utter a string of four-lettered words. "Sorry, you folks," Earrin added hastily. "I know this sort of thing bothers you, but the fact is that these people are trying to be scientific, and when you come right down to it I have to do the same to stay alive. I can't really blame them, except for hedging about it. The old words offend people, but they originally stood for common-sense actions. It's necessary to—pardon me—experiment in order to learn facts, and we need facts so as to be able to do the right things to stay alive."

"Then you agree with us!" one of the women exclaimed.

"No. I still believe Bones. I believe in some of your attitudes. I was taught the Faith in Surplus school, you know, and you can't expect someone who was aborted for the crime of being the third child born to his parents to feel much love for—"

"But they taught you how to live outside in that school, didn't they?"

"They taught me what to believe, not what to do. If I hadn't had the luck to meet another Nomad within a couple of days after being thrown out of Beehive, I'd have been a patch of slime on the Maine ricks thirteen years ago. Don't get me started on Surplus schools. My wife says pretty much the same about yours here at Great Blue. She only lived because she was older when she left, and there are a lot of jails around which she'd already had a chance to get to know. Now you characters are spoiling those."

"Making the air richer isn't spoiling them."

"Arranging that new Nomads will need three or four times normal oxygen concentration to behave rationally is certainly spoiling *them.*"

"But when the world gets back to normal, they'll be ready for it!"

Earrin, having no idea of the original composition of Earth's atmosphere, had no reply to this, but Mort did.

"The old atmosphere wasn't all oxygen. If you combine elementary chemistry with elementary arithmetic you find it couldn't have been more than a quarter. All you're likely to do if you try is run the total pressure up and make more trouble. To be all oxygen, you'll have to get rid of the nitrogen. Have you plans for that?"

Two of the young people laughed, and the discussion degenerated into noise while dogmatic statements flew back and forth.

Earrin kept silent; he liked Mort, but in spite of Bones' account he was not at all sure about the Hill dogma. He had grown up to treat all scientific terms as dirty words, but as he had come to learn what most of them meant—largely second-hand, from Kahvi's reading—he had realized that they described the policies he himself had to follow to keep alive. He did not, of course, stress this fact in his dealings with city-dwellers.

It was his fear of wasted action and time which finally caused Earrin to interrupt the polemic. It was increasingly obvious that neither side would convince the other.

"Save breath!" he called loudly, at last. "Mort, these kids have spent years convincing themselves that they're right. You're not going to talk them out of it. Even Bones couldn't talk them out of it, though he might possibly suggest experiments which would dent them. You others—Mort is a nice, devout Hiller, with lots of common sense buried in his devotion, and you're not going to get him to help with anything that goes against both the faith and the common sense. Find something else to argue about; arguments are a waste of time unless they're fun."

Neither party took this interruption very well, since Fyn had not been particularly tactful. Even Betty felt that her father had been unfairly described. The woman who had spoken before was also irritated; this may have caused her to use now a tactic which should certainly have been saved as a final resort.

"Mort, or whatever his name is, will be helping us whether he wants to or not. We have techniques which have worked before with parents—I suppose this is his child?"

"Yes," Fyn admitted unthinkingly, his habitual truthfulness once again overriding his common sense.

"I thought so. What's your name, young woman?"

"Betty—Betty Dent," the child replied.

"Betty, how would you like to spend the next few days, or maybe weeks, breathing really nice air—air that makes you feel smart and strong all the time?"

"You can't—" Mort started to snap, and Earrin also tensed as he saw what must be coming and connected it with the absence of his family.

"We can!" the woman cut in. "There are too

many of us here. You could stop us from getting her into a building, of course, but you don't have hands enough to keep all of us from her air hose. That could be pulled away very easily, couldn't it?''

"You couldn't—no one could do a thing like that!''

The woman shook her head. ''They all react the same. These idealists. They think no one would do what they can't bring themselves to do. No imagination. If the reasons are strong enough, a person can bring himself to do *anything*, no matter how unpleasant, Mort. We've found that out.''

"In an oxygen dream, I suppose.''

"That's right. Still no originality. First they don't believe, then they get insulting. Was it Betty's mother who went with Genda to spoil our air?''

"Yes." Mort could see nothing to be gained by denying the fact, though his conditioning against falsehood was not quite as overwhelming as Earrin's.

"Then we'll give you a while to decide. When she comes back we'll all tell her the situation. You can have fun while Genda explains why duty to the faith requires you both to defy us, and let Betty be turned into a—what's that nice insulting term?—an oxygen junky. You can assure each other that your child is too well brought up to yield to the awful temptation of breathing happily. You and your wife can argue with Genda—either way you like. We won't take Betty away just yet; it may be a while before there's any point in it.

The jail air may still be good, but I'm sure its plants have been spoiled by Genda and the other pure-nose, so maybe we couldn't convert Betty there, and she'd be in the way here in the lab. She might even cause damage, as your Invader did in the other one—throwing critical cultures around like an animal!

"But let's keep the rules clear, Mort. You and your family will stay around here until you decide to help the work. If you try to leave, especially to go back to the city, a certain air hose will be in danger. We oxygen-wasters are going to make sure that the oxygen in the jail isn't wasted—except, of course, for a couple who will stay outside to see that you behave. You may go out to Earrin's raft, of course, if there's enough air for you there. You two—" she indicated two of the largest men in her group—"stay outside for a while. Keep close to the young lady—*she's* not to go out to the raft—and make sure none of these people does anything I wouldn't like. I'll send someone out to take your places before we've breathed up too much of what's still there. Come on, you others."

Earrin interrupted the group's departure.

"I suppose this is an old trick of yours, as you say. Does that mean you have my wife and daughter hidden away somewhere, too?"

The woman turned back to him, and the rest of the group stopped to listen. "No," she said without hesitation. "They don't seem to have been on your raft all day. We looked and could tell you had a child there, but neither it nor your wife has been seen. We've had work parties all over the peninsula and even on the islands gathering material for the lab here, and none of them saw anyone. We had a guard on your raft for a while, to be honest—" she tilted her head at one of her companions—"but he got sick and had to come ashore. Wherever your wife is, she went of her own free will, if you can trust those monsters you associate with."

"And if I can trust your word," Earrin returned pointedly. The woman made no response to this, and a minute later all but the two guards, Earrin, Mort, and Betty had disappeared. There was an indistinct sound of voices from the jail, and then Zhamia and Genda emerged. The latter appeared highly indignant, the expression being partly concealed by her mask and clearly revealed by her body set.

A few words brought both parties more or less up to date. The women had seeded about two thirds of the oxygen plants in the jail, but it would take a day or two for the new organisms to take over. None of this, however, was going to prevent the young Hillers from running things as they pleased, the part of the situation which bothered Earrin the most. He growled this fact aloud, and Mort agreed glumly.

"I don't see what we can do about it, though," the teacher added.

"How about that animal who hid in the water?" Genda asked. "I suppose there's no way it can be useful." Fyn ignored the implied contempt, and answered slowly.

"I was just wondering about that," he said. "This version of Bones isn't very large, but—you know, he does have a certain advantage. I'll have to thank that bossy female for reminding me of it. You folks wait here; I expect he's in or under the raft, and I want to talk to him before it's too dark to read signals." Without waiting for agreement, Earrin plunged into the water. The two guards had heard the conversation and looked rather uneasy, but couldn't decide on any action. The orders, after all, had been definite that the prisoners could visit the raft if they chose. Of course, there had not at that time been any suggestion that one of the Invaders might be there—

They drew a little apart from the others and talked in a low tone. Even Genda made no effort to listen in. The wait was brief. Earrin reappeared in waist-deep water, and the Observer popped up beside him almost at once. The two waded ashore and approached the guards. They stopped within two meters of the pair, and Earrin spoke.

"This is the Invader, as you call him, that you folks held prisoner for a long time in Hemenway. He didn't much like the things you did to him. He is not violent by nature, being intelligent, but he agrees with me that it would be a waste of effort to inconvenience ourselves very greatly to keep people like you breathing."

"He's too small to worry about," retorted one of the guards. "What could he do to a grown man?"

"That depends on the environment, as people so often say," replied Earrin. "Your leader just pointed out one of the possibilities to me. In a fight

where muscular strength was the key, I agree
you'd have him recaptured in no time. However,
he has the rest of us to help him, and one big
advantage which might make that help unnecessary."

"What's that?"

"He doesn't have to breathe—in fact, he can't.
He has no vulnerable air lines. If you fight with
him, what do you think you could do to keep those
ropy arms from pulling *your* hoses in the first ten
seconds? Want to try?" Earrin paused for a few
seconds to let his audience think. "If you do, start
in. We find it inconvenient, as I said a moment
ago, to have our actions restrained by you people.
If you think a fight would be impractical, get inside that jail with the rest of your junky friends,
and tell them that any head sticking out of the
water gets its hose pulled loose instantly. Think
fast."

They thought, though not very fast. They expos-
tulated. They even begged; it seemed that facing
their termagant leader under the circumstances
was almost as frightening as losing their masks.
Earrin was not at all sure that he could, in fact
carry out his threat; but Bones probably could,
and in any case it seemed that the young Hillers
were in no position to doubt his word. He was not
lying; he fully intended to do what he had said.

The two finally went through the air lock. A
renewed babble of voices sounded inside the jail;
though words could not be made out very well,
most of the listeners who could do so grinned
behind their masks.

Then there was a brief silence, and rather to Earrin's surprise a head popped out of the water. The Nomad did not have to test his firmness; Bones reacted instantly. A tentacle whipped out, its four-fingered tip seized the air hose and jerked. The tube pulled away from its cartridge but not from the mask; the latter left its wearer. There was a glimpse of furious female features, and the head disappeared under water again. A moment later shrieks could be heard from inside the jail; apparently the woman lacked the hangup about keeping unprotected eyes closed under water. Even very dilute nitric acid can hurt. Fyn felt nauseated, the other human listeners went pale, and Betty started to cry. Their efforts to calm her helped the rest to resign themselves to the unpleasant situation.

"We've got them," Mort remarked thoughtfully when the child was quiet again. "Now just what do we do with them?"

The question was unanswered hours later, when the oxygen wasters had presumably gone happily to sleep inside the jail, and Kahvi and her companions arrived.

JANET AULISIO

XVIII

Variations, Violent

The moon was up by this time, and there was
enough light for human beings and Observers to
signal each other, but the latter wasted no time on
gestures at first. They flung themselves into each
other's tentacles and embraced for fully a minute,
while memories transferred themselves. Even
Earrin, who had come to understand the situation
pretty well, was embarrassed to watch—though
watch he did. The other adults were shocked,
though Kahvi recovered quickly when her husband explained. The burning need for population
control immediately after the change, coupled
with the collapse of all but pseudolife technology,

247

had restored a decidedly Victorian behavior code, with much less hypocrisy than had characterized that age.

The Observers knew all that had happened to each other within two minutes; it took much longer for words to bring to human minds a more or less uniform and up-to-date picture of the situation. The moon was a good deal higher by then.

Action was promptly initiated by Kahvi.

"Now we bring those creatures back to normal air," she said positively.

"How?" asked Zhamia. "We've seeded their plants, but it will take a couple of days before the oxygen producers are really overcome by the N-seed. If there aren't enough nitrates in the trays, the seeding may not work at all. And we haven't been into this new place—the lab, they called it; they must have straight oxygen there, too."

Kahvi smiled grimly inside her mask. "There's wild cartridge tissue around. These folks have either been careless with pseudolife fragments or have been growing things deliberately all over the peninsula. We'll get a couple of chunks of that into the buildings, or at least the one where they are now; that'll bring the oxygen pressure down to standard in half an hour!"

"Do you think the roof will stand it?" asked Earrin. Kahvi thought for a moment.

"Sure," she said at last. "The wall is only a few centimeters into the air lock pool. The pressure drop will lower the water outside until bubbles can come in, before the roof tissue fails."

"Even with fresh patches?"

"We'll hope so." Fyn was startled; he had never

seen his wife in such a ruthless mood. He had not seen their child studded with glass caltrops either. "They have masks, anyway," Kahvi added.

"One of them doesn't—the boss, I think. Bones pulled it off when she tried to—"

"Yes, you told us. All right, put it back inside. Don't leave the lock; just put it by the edge of the water. If they're asleep we don't want them to wake up. We can do that later if it's necessary—but why should it be? The oxygen pressure will only go down to normal. You aren't thinking."

"Is normal enough for them?" asked Earrin.

"They make do with it in the city. Stop being so sympathetic, or if you must be, get sympathetic about Danna and me. We still hurt where that scientific glass went in." Her husband, deciding not to explain that he was still worried about the roof, ceased arguing and went off for a supply of cartridge tissue. Mort and Betty followed; the child had never seen this kind of pseudolife, and her father could not reasonably overlook a chance at her education, tired as they were.

The other children were taken to the raft and nested down by Kahvi. She was back ashore long before the three got back with the needed material.

To anyone familiar with Terrestrial plants when there were any, it would have looked like a section of bamboo almost as long as Earrin was tall, and fully the length of his forearm in diameter. Its bright red color was not obvious by moonlight. It was light enough to carry easily under one arm; and in fact, Betty had carried it with a little trouble from almost the end of the peninsula. It would be over a hundred kilograms heavier when saturated with oxygen, but this could not happen outdoors. There were traces of the gas still free in Earth's atmosphere, but even white phosphorus would not have been affected by it.

"Good!" exclaimed Kahvi as she saw the mass of tissue. "You only found one? Well, that'll be enough; they're all in the jail, and that'll certainly eat a jailful of oxy—and it isn't as though we were using it up, either. We can't get it in dry, but that won't slow it much. Let's go; it's certainly light enough."

It was actually much too light; Kahvi couldn't submerge it. An object which displaces around a hundred liters of water and weighs less than two kilograms will easily float a sixty-five kilogram person who is herself only a little more dense than water and loaded with breathing gear. Kahvi needed help. Eventually, all the adults working together managed to lever one end of the cylinder under the wall, and by united and coordinated pushing worked it through until it popped to the surface on the inside. There was no sound to suggest that it had been noticed.

Then Zhamia took her daughter out to the raft, returning in a few minutes. It had been decided that only the children should occupy the tent until after sunrise, when the oxygen plants would resume activity. The adults stayed on guard around the air lock of the jail, most of them sleeping on the slimy sand.

Kahvi and Earrin stayed awake, watching the water level of the air lock. This should have been going down as the pressure inside dropped; but nothing of the sort seemed to be happening as the minutes passed. Both knew that time appears to go slowly during periods of anticipation, but finally the comet rose.

"It should have shown something by now!" exclaimed Kahvi. "I wonder what's gone wrong?"

"Maybe the stuff has altered, and isn't binding oxygen. You can't really go by looks, you know."

The woman didn't even bother to nod agreement; that was the most obvious of the possibilities. Even pseudolife, stable as it was compared to real-life, sometimes altered its genetic pattern cancerwise. "I'm going inside," the woman said suddenly. "Something's wrong, and they must be too sound asleep to notice."

"I'll go." Earrin seldom actually overruled his wife with any success, except when he was right. She did not argue this time, but settled thankfully down to rest again. The man waded down the steps and ducked under the wall.

It was easy to see inside. The moon was high, and the light panels helped where it failed to reach. The tables which bore the planters prevented direct view of most of the room until Earrin was up the inside stairs, but he could see one man standing, unmasked, near the west wall and watching the Nomad enter. In the moonlight it took a few seconds to recognize Rembert, the first of the oxygen addicts he and Kahvi had met. The presence of this particular waster, however, was far less surprising than the fact that he was entirely alone. No other human being was in the room.

"I'm glad to see you, Nomad Fyn," the Hiller said calmly. "I'm also glad that you weren't badly hurt when I pulled your feet from under you the other afternoon. I'm afraid I over-reacted at the idea you were associating with an Invader."

"Where did—?" Earrin didn't have to finish the question. Rembert smiled broadly, and nodded toward the southwest corner of the jail. The Nomad followed the indication with his eyes, but at first saw nothing meaningful. The walls were solid, and certainly there could not be an air lock of some unheard-of design—an airtight double door, or something of that sort. The craftsmanship involved in such stone work would be incredible, and the wall *was* of stone; Fyn had climbed it, and knew.

Then he saw the roof. For seconds he could not credit what his eyes were telling him, but they insisted. Clearly visible in the moonlight, a finger's length from the south and west walls and extending nearly a meter along each from the corner where they met, was a row of square patches, each slightly overlapping the next.

"This tissue grows rapidly, too," Rembert remarked happily. "I'm sure you'd be glad to have some of the culture."

"You—cut—the—roof—open." The Nomad could barely get the words out.

"That's right. I patched it right up again, though, when everyone else had gotten out. They were very kind. They went as fast as they could without making noise, so I wouldn't lose much oxygen. I must say the level seems low now, though. There was more exchange through the hole than I expected; I must say I don't see why. There was quite a breeze in through the opening, but that didn't make sense."

Earrin, still far too shocked to speak, nodded

toward the cylinder of cartridge tissue floating on the water of the lock, still bobbing from his own passage. Rembert looked puzzled, and Fyn at last found enough voice to explain.

"It's the stuff that goes in breathing cartridges. If the oxygen around it is above a certain concentration it soaks it up; if lower, it gives it off. I'm surprised you never learned about it."

"I never bothered to go outside until recently. My friends taught me how to use a mask, but didn't mention all those details." Fyn restrained himself from the obvious remark about the friends, and changed the subject.

"Why didn't you leave with the others?"

"Why, Earrin! I'm surprised at you! Someone had to patch the roof, obviously. I volunteered because of course I expected to have the whole roomful of oxygen to myself after they were gone. I didn't count on your rather unfair trick with that awful tissue. We'll have to develop one with a higher equilibrium, for interim use."

"And your friends deserted you here?"

"Oh, they'll be back, with others. You didn't really expect to keep us fooled, or in your power, for very long, did you?"

"Why not? The natives are still with us. Even if you bring a lot of help, they can still—"

"Didn't your alien friend tell you about the unpleasant things we can do? You really haven't come to appreciate all the uses of edged and pointed tools, my friend."

Earrin made no answer to this. Bones had by now told him about the spears and glass splinters.

He could not blame himself or Kahvi for not foreseeing the escape; the method used was com-

pletely unthinkable to any Nomad. Even city
dwellers would not normally have wasted air so
grossly. These youngsters, however, seemed to
have made a major break with everything Earrin
regarded as natural and proper. Since these included normal methods of self-preservation, it
didn't seem likely that the group could last long;
but they could be dangerous while they did.

If several dozen, or perhaps a hundred, of them
came back to the jail with those weapons, they
would be in control again at once. Even if the
human enemies could improvise foot protection,
it was hard to see what could be done for the
walking-tentacles of the natives; and while the
latter seemed able to survive spears, the human
opponents could not. There was nothing which
could be fashioned into shields—that concept
came more naturally to Fyn than it had to
Bones—since the local realwood was available
only in narrow strips rather than boards. Wick-
erwork did not occur to him, and would have
been dismissed as inadequate and too time con-
suming if it had.

All this musing, he told himself abruptly, was
futile. They were all in danger. Kahvi and the
others had to be warned, and the children taken
out of reach of the menace. Duty or not, if the little
ones fell into the hands of these me-first
youngsters, Earrin knew he would obey orders.

"Breathe easy," he said suddenly and automatically to Rembert, and ducked through the air
lock.

Kahvi couldn't believe his report until she had
climbed to the roof to examine it for herself. Once
convinced, however, she thought rapidly.

"We could get the raft out of their reach easily enough; they can't be back for hours yet. The trouble is that there isn't air for all of us in the tent, and won't be even after the sun comes up. It would take the plants a day or more to grow enough new leaf surface. It looks as though you others will have to get back to the city quickly with your children."

"We could take yours, too," pointed out Zhamia.

"No, thanks." Kahvi was emphatic, but offered no reasons. "It's a pity to wake them up; they've had a hard night already. I don't see any—"

"It would really be a pity, as you say," Rembert's voice interrupted. None of them had seen him emerge from the jail; they had been far too concerned with their own problems. "Do you really suppose we were so stupid as to allow you that chance? Only one person went back to Hemenway for help; the others are watching from the ridge. If you try to take your children past them to the city, you will certainly regret it. You may as well let them sleep. As you suggest, nothing more is likely to happen before morning. Please explain all this to your Invader friends, too; they may not have understood me clearly, and it would be a pity if they annoyed us."

Fyn was already gesturing to the two Boneses, and getting response. Rembert could not understand the responses, of course, but seemed unworried by the fact. He was as sure that his side was in power as Kahvi and Earrin had been about theirs so shortly before. Rembert couldn't see what the others might do; that was enough for him.

But even Earrin, slow-witted as he was, saw

what might be done—background information, not brilliance, made the difference. The first thing was to get the children out of the Hillers' reach— he included automatically the two who were not his own. He gave little thought about what would happen to himself and adult companions; there was always the city, which had plenty of air in spite of Genda's ideas. Obviously, one or both of the natives should take the raft out of reach of the Hillers as soon as possible. Earrin gestured this, together with his reasons, to his duplicate friends.

Bones, of course, were reluctant to go. There was much more to be seen right where they were. However, they had recently embraced, and it was logical that they separate so that more could be observed. Equally logically, the larger unit would be able to move the raft faster; and finally, the same one would be producing a bud in a day or two as a result of the spear wound. It seemed advisable that this occur out of reach of the Hillers. Bones therefore agreed that the larger unit would depart at once with the raft and children and take them as far as Milton, far enough for reasonable safety and near enough for quick return.

Earrin approved this decision, but made the mistake of translating it to Zhamia and the others; like most people of his time he was totally unused to direct conflict, couldn't see what Rembert could do about the matter, and made no effort to keep the oxygen-waster from hearing. Even Kahvi didn't spot the error until too late. Rembert, unfortunately, was both a quick thinker and dedicated to his cause.

He could not travel as fast as Bones, but was not far behind the native in reaching the raft. The others followed when they saw where he was going, but failed to guess soon enough what he had in mind—again, it was something unthinkable for most of them, in spite of recent experience.

The junky climbed rather clumsily onto the deck and made his way across the floats to the tent. Then, quite calmly, he drew a glass knife from his harness pouch and held it close to the transparent tissue. Even his voice was calm.

"I know you or your Invader can pull my hose," he said. "You can't do it fast enough, though. Want to take the chance, Nomad, before I slash your tent open? Think your kids would wake up soon enough to get masks on, even if you started yelling right now? Come a step closer, or make a loud noise, and one tentful of air is gone. In fact, since I can't hold the knife out like this all night, you'd better get off the raft altogether and back ashore—all of you. I can count, even in air this thin. That goes for both your Invaders, too. I know one of them is under water. Go after him, one of you who can talk to him, and get him ashore too. I'll wait right here until my friends come, and you'll wait right there by the lab until they do. You'd better get your Invader fast; I can see the entry hole inside your tent, and if his head comes up through it I use the knife."

"You wouldn't dare," gritted Kahvi. "Can you guess what we'd do to you?"

"Sure. I knew some people would get killed in this operation. It's worth it, even if I didn't really expect to be one of them."

"You can't—"

"Do you really want to take that chance? *Get off this raft*, right now!"

Bones had submerged to get an anchor, and came up with it at this point. Earrin quickly transmitted an explanation of the new status, though the Observer could evaluate it pretty well without help. It was another fascinating situation, forcing reconsideration of all current hypotheses about individual-mind behavior. Logically, one should challenge the threat of the individual with the knife in order to determine how closely its sound codes corresponded to actual mental activity; but now that it was necessary to attach so much value to individual lives, that experiment would have to wait. It was a pity; the situation could obviously not be repeated *without* any lives in danger. It seemed best to obey instructions and go ashore with the rest. That would give time for thought. Rembert watched the company gather on the beach, counted it carefully, and relaxed.

Slowly the moon sank westward, the comet rose toward the meridian, and the eastern sky grew brighter. The people ashore were very tired, but could not sleep. They couldn't be sure whether the junky was bluffing, but couldn't face the risk; all of them but Genda had children under threat, and even she did not want to risk them. They could plan all they wished without being overheard by Rembert, for the surf made far too much noise to let him hear voices at that distance. Unfortunately, there seemed no worthwhile plan.

The status held until sunrise. Zhamia was the first to see the group of people approaching over the ridge from the west; they had been expected from the south, of course. The reason was quickly obvious; they had spread out so that none of the group by the laboratory could retreat in any direction except toward the water.

About three quarters of the fifty or sixty newcomers had spears. These were not actually levelled, but by the time the group had reached the beach and surrounded the Nomads and their friends at a distance of only four or five meters, the impression of threat was as great as if they had been. Facial expressions could not be seen, but body attitudes were plain enough. Action supported them almost instantly.

"You Nomads, and the people with you, get away from those Invaders." The female voice was quite recognizable; Earrin wished he knew her name. He hesitated, then stepped aside as ordered, followed by the other human beings. He regretted it at once.

"All right, get them!" the same voice ordered. Half a dozen of the weapons instantly flew at the Observers. Their owners must have been concentrating on the more difficult target, for the larger unit went untouched, while four of the weapons lodged in the body of the smaller. It snatched at the shafts with wildly thrashing tentacles, and one by one pulled them out. Colorless blood spurted from the wounds, and the Observer staggered a meter or two toward the water before it fell.

The Hillers watched silently, throwing no more missiles until Bones moved; but as the larger unit snatched up the smaller body and plunged toward the waves, several more points had to be dodged.

JANET AULISIO

XIX

Mystery, Metallic

Once out of sight below the surface, Bones made straight out from the shore for a couple of hundred meters. The smaller unit was a helpless burden, but as they travelled, they transferred ideas. There was no question of total destruction; vital organs of the Observer units were too well decentralized for such injuries to be fatal. Fairly complete dissection, or incineration, would have been needed for that.

They reached a large patch of marine weed, and Bones left the other there to eat and heal. The idea was that it would remain for two full days before acting on its own; if possible, the larger unit would return with newer knowledge by that time.

The next goal was the raft. This must be done quickly, too, the Observer reflected; the newcomers could be expected to do something about the buds as quickly as possible. It seemed likely that Rembert would have relaxed his attention now that his friends had arrived, but it would be necessary to check carefully—yes, there was a human figure wading shoreward from the raft. Bones took the chance of emerging briefly at the seaward end of the vessel to make sure that no one else was on deck. A second or two later the odd head came up into the tent.

The children were still asleep, in spite of the noise on the beach. The larger ones would obviously not know the gesture language; whether little Danna could be made to understand the situation, and communicate it in time to the others, was a matter for worry. Bones had known the child's limitations long before the reason for them had become clear.

Without climbing into the tent—even standing on the bottom, the Observer's head nearly reached its top—Bones reached into Danna's nest and gently pressed her shoulder. It was the standard please-pay-attention symbol, which one could hope would get through to the sleeping mind. The four fingers at the end of the long tentacle squeezed, and waited; squeezed again; again. The noise ashore grew louder, and Bones swivelled an eyeball in that direction. There seemed to be no motion toward the raft, but the people were now so closely grouped together that action of individuals could not be made out even by Observer eyesight.

Another squeeze on the tiny shoulder brought results. Danna sat up, rubbed her eyes, and looked calmly up at her nonhuman friend.

"Where are Mother and Dad?" A tentacle gestured shoreward; the child looked that way and nodded. She did not seem frightened at the bustle, and turned back to Bones. "Are they all right? What's happening?" The Observer did not think of hiding any information, but gestured as swiftly as possible.

"I can't tell whether your parents are all right. The other people are the ones your mother ran from last night, and their friends. She thinks they want to take you from her, and hurt you unless she does what they want. You and these other small ones will have to get your masks on and come with me. Take all the air you can carry. I will take you to one of the tents across the bay, where these people can't get to you. Wake up the others and explain to them as quickly as you can."

The first part of this instruction was easy to carry out, but convincing the other children that they should go anywhere with the strange giant was quite another matter. Since Danna was so obviously on friendly terms with it they were not actually afraid—or at least, didn't want to show fear in front of their younger companion—but going into the sea where eyes were so little use made both of them uneasy. Both, fortunately, had heard enough the night before to make them afraid of the Hemenway group—Ray in particular recalled the incident at the other jail; but they agreed to go only after Danna had convinced them that travelling in the water with Bones was fun.

Even then they were not really enthusiastic, until an emphatic tentacle gesture toward the shore directed their attention to the fact that people were wading toward them. Then all reached for their breathing equipment.

Danna, true to her training, checked everyone's mask and cartridges before they entered the water, though the others were becoming uneasy as the crowd approached.

"All right," the little girl said finally. "Bones will hold on to you, and I'll hold onto him—I know how, but you might get pulled off when he goes fast. Hold those extra cartridges carefully, remember. Let's go." Danna had gestured briefly to Bones that he was to keep hold of the others, and within a few seconds the group was away from the raft and, presumably, safe from the delinquents. Ray and Betty were tucked under a fin on each side, held firmly by the long tentacles; Danna was pressed against the dorsal surface of the fishlike form holding firmly to the roots of the same limbs, just below Bones' eyes.

The Observer was slowed, of course, by the triple burden, but was still travelling faster than any human being could swim. This did not make the children safe, however; they had to be brought to some place where they could breathe before their cartridges ran out, and all nearby places were likely to be visited by the *enemy*—another concept new to the Observer, but growing clearer with experience.

There were places where they would be safe; Earrin and Kahvi had several tents around the Boston area. Whether any of them could be reached with a safe air margin was very uncertain. Bones had no way of judging how long the supply carried by the children would last. Swimming speed was far below normal, and the trip even to the nearest would be long.

But there was a way to increase the speed, the Observer suddenly realized. The children were not aware of the sudden change of course as the idea burgeoned. Bones felt it was safe to pass between the Sayre islands and the mainland, since the fugitives would not be visible under water and there was no obvious reason for the Hillers to be crossing the channel. The error of this belief turned out to be unimportant, since no one was getting structural materials from the island at the time, and they got through the strait, around the north end of the peninsula, and into the bay where Kahvi had come ashore with her daughter. Danna recognized the spot where they landed, and showed the other children the things her mother had explained, while the Observer went to work.

The big mass of Newell tissue was still there. There were plenty of cordage growths. Bones, using the glass knife from Danna's pouch, hacked off a slab with little trouble; it cut like the foamed plastic of long before which had inspired its genetic design. In a quarter of an hour it had been shaped roughly into a flat-topped boat, or perhaps a surfboard, and rigged with tow-lines for the Observer and holds for the passengers. At a gesture, the latter carried it to the water; another, and Danna laughed.

"Hold on tight," he said to the others. "We're going to go very fast."

They did. They went around the north side of the Sayre islands, and turned east. The children weren't quite sure whether to enjoy the experience or be frightened, but tiny Danna's complete trust in Bones influenced the others.

They crossed the bay and passed south of Milton island. There was an air tent there, and Bones had debated using it; but the family had restocked it recently with a new variety of pseudolife, and had planned to treat it as an emergency site only until the changed system reached its new equilibrium. It seemed safer to go on to Copper. This took them past the northern end of the Blue Hills, slightly southward, and after some ten kilometers of swimming, to the island which had once been Penn's Hill. The tent here was well established. It was the family home while they were gathering copper.

The source lay about a kilometer and a half to the east, under forty meters of water, at the site of the former Fore River shipyard. Here the copper-isolating pseudolife forms still delivered their nuggets, unimpressed by the fact that the still-melting pole caps had rendered the area accessible only to Bones.

The Observer made sure the children entered the home, checked the water level of the air lock, helped Danna make sure of the condition of the air plants, watched her set out all their cartridges to charge, and left them eating happily. Leaving the boat drawn up where they had landed, Bones headed back at full speed toward the Canton shore.

Now completely unhampered, the powerful body made the distance in little more than ten minutes. The last kilometer was done entirely submerged, but there was no difficulty in finding the raft, and the grotesque head emerged carefully into the air tent.

There was one person inside, working on the plants with ordinary Nomad attention to important business. She had her back to the hatch, and it was some seconds before she saw the Observer. When she did, she made no sound or gesture, but there was no trouble divining the question in Kahvi Mikkonen's mind. Bones answered it.

"Danna and the other children are at Copper, with all the air and food they need. I can get them back quickly when you wish. What has happened to Earrin?" Kahvi frowned.

"They are using him as they wanted to use the children. I still find it hard to believe that they'll really—really kill him, but they say they will unless you come back and let them talk to you. I don't see how they could expect you to go near them, after what they did a few hours ago; but they felt sure you'd come back to the raft, and told me to wait here and give you the message. I can't

ask you to give up your life for my Earrin, though;
he can't mean that much to you."

Bones thought deeply. The concepts of death
and killing were fairly clear now; it could be seen
why they meant more to human beings than pain
or even ignorance. As with Kahvi, the belief that
Earrin's life was really in danger from his own
species could not really lodge in the Observer's
mind, though the emotional and conceptual block
involved was of course different from the woman's.

With the other Observer unit out of action for
hours yet, Bones was unwilling to risk serious
damage to this one, much less its complete
destruction—a possibility, since the Hillers obviously had access to fire. Once the other unit
healed, of course, the Observer would certainly
consider risking a body in the hands of people as
long as the other could watch what occurred; but
until then, Bones did not want to take serious
chances.

"You say they just want to talk to me, now?" the
native gestured at this point in its thoughts.

"That's what they say. Maybe they mean it.
They did want to find out how to kill you people,
and maybe they're satisfied about that, now.
Maybe you can believe them."

"Of course. Surely they must know their own
intentions."

The possibility of a deliberate lie had still not
really dawned on the nonhuman mind. Kahvi, in
view of recent experience, seriously considered

trying to explain, but decided against it. It seemed easier to advise Bones to play things safely.

"You could talk to them, if all they really want is that," she pointed out. "They may not all have the same ideas, remember; but if you stay out here on the raft, and have those who want to talk come out wading without their spears, they would know you could get away under water before they could possibly hurt you. Why don't I suggest that to them? If they agree, we can believe that talk is really all they want."

"That seems sensible," replied the Observer. "I would like to talk to them, also. I know their theory about my responsibility for the air change; I can tell them this is wrong, and perhaps glean from their memories, if the speech code is really specific enough, some clues as to what did really happen. I realize there are no intact memories left even though there were human units here at the time, because of your incredibly indirect communication."

"That seems to be about it," admitted Kahvi, "as far as I can make out from what these delinquents told Earrin and me. You realize, I hope, that your way of direct memory transfer between bodies is just as incredible to us; we think of your two units as two people."

"That is coming to me. In any case, while I do know that one of your theories is wrong—I did *not* do anything to your air, and did not come here until it was as it is now—I do not know what is right, and wish very much to find out. It always seems to happen, on world after world. The air is always like this when we arrive—otherwise we wouldn't arrive—but close investigation always indicates that at some earlier time there was indeed much free oxygen. There always seems to have been life adapted to such a condition—inevitably; oxygen is far too active to be in an atmosphere for long without life forms to maintain the supply." Kahvi nodded; basic biochemistry was part of even Nomad education. "It seems reasonable to infer that the ordinary course of evolution eventually produced an organism, probably microscopic in size and rapidly reproducing, which oxidized nitrogen; but inference is of course not knowledge by itself."

"You sometimes have to act as though it were," the woman remarked.

"That seems to be true for you *individuals*," admitted Bones. "You lack the time to let inferences accumulate and check against reality until they become knowledge. However that may be, the same change seems to have occurred on all the worlds I have seen. An organism develops which oxidizes nitrogen with free oxygen, and a new equilibrium is reached between the two—the one this world has now, with only a trace of free oxygen."

"The story is that men made the organism. We know they made many—most of the ones which keep us alive now are artificial," Kahvi agreed. "I can't see, though, why they'd make one which destroyed the air, except by mistake; and how could anyone make such a mistake? They would have had to think, first, surely. That's why most of the Nomads we know doubt that the world ever did have oxygen in its air."

"It did," Bones assured her. "I made the usual tests when I landed. There are no symbols in our mutual language to explain them, but I feel quite sure of *that* inference." Kahvi of course accepted the statement, and thought deeply for some seconds. She had not forgotten her husband and daughter, but was hoping that this problem, if it could be solved, might affect relations with the group she now called the Delinquents.

"You must know," she said at last, "what sort of life form does oxidize the nitrogen. Is it a pseudolife of the sort people made, or nitro-life like yours which is most of what grows now?"

"It is nitro-life," the Observer replied. "There are a large number of species. However, much of the pseudolife you use is of the same variety. It would seem possible that artificial life made by your people was indeed responsible for the change."

"But pseudolife is so stable, and nitro-life mutates so easily!"

"Which is why a single mistake on the part of your life technicians could have sufficed."

"I'd hate to have Genda turn out to be right. She's bad enough to listen to now," Kahvi muttered. Bones did not understand this in the least, and waited for something answerable. It came.

"You know how pseudolife is made—you could make it yourself."

"Yes."

"Could you make any of the kinds which oxidize nitrogen?"

"Yes."

"Would it be more difficult than making other kinds, or might it happen by accident?"

"It could hardly happen by accident. All the organisms able to do this, on every world I remember, use one or another of four enzymes—you know what they are?"

"Of course. The symbol is plain enough; we've talked about such things in our own life systems."

"Those enzymes use a very surprising metal."

"What's surprising about it?"

"I have not been able to learn why it is so widespread in every planet's crust. It is one of the standing mysteries, which presents itself on world after world. It is a highly unreactive metal, which I would expect to find uncombined and highly localized. It should *not* be so thoroughly spread through a planet's soil and crust that a microbe can count on finding enough of its atoms whenever it needs them for its personal chemistry. One hypothesis is that a scientific race used and scattered it, but there has been no way to tell; I have never found a use for it myself, except in the most limited quantities in the laboratory. That is one reason I want to talk to these people of yours who seem to be somewhat scientific in nature. They might have knowledge of their own, even if memories are gone."

Kahvi had her doubts about this; she felt that she knew pretty accurately the scientific status of the Delinquents. Essentially, they had probably been playing with cultures and Evolution Plant enzymes on a hit-or-miss basis. However, that was Bones' problem.

"What is this metal?" she asked. "Some obscure heavy element they never mentioned either in Surplus School or Citizen's Training, I suppose."

"You know about it," Bones replied. A handling tentacle reached out and touched the gold bracelet on her left wrist.

XX

Answers, Applied

If one of the Delinquents, or even an ordinary Hiller, had said it, Kahvi might have doubted; but Bones was Bones. Nomads merely regarded lying as hopelessly immoral; Bones didn't know what it was, since it was impossible in her natural method of communication. A human being might have been honestly wrong; Bones *knew*.

There *had* been an Earth with a breathable atmosphere—

And millions and millions of people—

A slow grin spread over Kahvi's face. Her lip trembled, and she suddenly burst into laughter;

peal after peal of uncontrollable laughter. Bones
was familiar with this manifestation of the
human nervous system's reaction to incongruity,
but was mystified by the lack of any obvious incongruity this time. Kahvi, when she could finally
stop, was little help.

"I'd like to be translating, or at least standing
there, when you tell that to Genda and Rembert's
crowd at the same time!" was all she said.

"Why won't you be?" was the natural question.

"We can't leave the kids out at Copper that long.
I'd trust Danna, but the other two are older and
will have to show her they're smarter, sometime
or other. We can hope they're reasonably safe so
far, but that won't last more than a few hours if
nothing happens to them." She paused to think
for a moment. "Here's what we'll do. I'll go ashore
and tell the Delinquents that you've come back
and are willing to talk, and that you've put the
kids 'way out of their reach. I'll tell them that you
know just what happened to the world's air—"

"But I don't!" objected the Observer, startled.

"But you certainly do. A hundred million—a
billion—ten billion—whatever it was—people
like me wearing gold ornaments. Jewelry. That's
what spread the metal over the world so well. It's
obvious. It wasn't your doing, it wasn't science's
doing. Can't you just see Genda and those young
devils having to admit to each other that they're
both wrong?" Neither Kahvi nor Bones had any
grasp of the basic human skill at avoiding any
such admission. "I'll tell 'em you know, and that
you'll explain to everyone who wants to listen at,

say, sunrise tomorrow. That will give them plenty of time to fetch all the people they want, and give you plenty of time to get me out to Copper and come back again. When you do explain, they won't have any more reason to kill you; it obviously doesn't matter to you what the air is like, and they should be able to see that. That will mean you have no reason for interfering in their attempt to change it back. Oh!"

"What?"

"One of them was saying—you were captured in a room in Hemenway with a lot of plants and things?"

"Yes."

"You smashed some of the planters?"

"I threw one at people who were throwing spears at me."

"Why did you pick that one?"

"It was nearest."

"I hope you can convince them. I gather it was a culture of whatever they are planning to change the air back—something that will reduce nitrates very fast. I don't know what it uses for energy. That fellow was sure you'd tried to destroy it on purpose." She thought for some seconds. "I still can't come up with anything better. Can you?"

"No," admitted Bones. "In any case, we should start your trip to Copper. I suggest you go to tell those people what you can. I will make another boat, of the sort I carried the children on; it will save much time in the long run. I'll be back with it shortly. If they'll let you come with me, fine; if not, we'll have to think of something else. If necessary,

I will go back and bring the children here; they would be safer, I suppose, even with these other people around."

"I'm afraid so. We'll try this, though." Kahvi got dressed and slid through the hatchway. Bones followed, watched her for a moment as she stood up and began to wade toward the group on the shore, and then dolphined at top speed toward the north and the supply of Newell tissue.

Half an hour later the slab of solid foam came bobbing back into view of the jail area. Kahvi, rather to Bones' surprise, was waiting in waist-deep water; she clambered onto the crudely streamlined float, and the native promptly headed eastward again.

She looked back several times, but had to give most of her attention to holding on; the board literally bounced from wave to wave at times. She wondered how the children had managed—surely Bones hadn't travelled this fast with them! No worry; there had been no mention of losing any, and Bones had said that they—plural, definitely—were safe at Copper.

But there were worries at both ends of the trip. Had the youngsters done anything dangerous? She could trust her own daughter, but didn't know the others very well. And what was happening to Earrin, in the hands of the Delinquents? She gave another look aft, and gasped.

Smoke was rising from the jail area—it seemed to be the jail area—her eyes and her mask window wouldn't let her be certain. It had to be smoke; the sky was cloudless, and it was rising visibly. What had happened? Was Earrin safe? She strained her eyes, but could make out nothing more, and was drawing away from the scene as the seconds passed. Should she go back? What would happen to the children if she did? Maybe Bones could see better, and tell her what was going on.

She jerked repeatedly on the tow harness, but the water was far too choppy to let the Observer tell one tug on the rope from another, and she was swimming entirely under water. The Canton shore and the smoke slowly faded astern, and finally disappeared around the Blue Hills peninsula. Kahvi settled for looking ahead.

The children were safe. After a single glance had made this clear, Kahvi frantically passed the new information to the native. Bones was about to plunge back into the water to go back to Canton; she barely stopped the dive.

"What do you want?" asked the Observer. "I can get back much more quickly alone, and bring word back to you."

"But you wouldn't know what has happened to Earrin! Those young monsters said they'd kill him if anything went wrong, and obviously something's wrong! They might blame him, or me, for whatever made the smoke."

"Do you wish to come back and leave these young ones?"

"Yes!—No—I don't know—the children could still—"

"Your husband can probably take care of himself without you better than they can."

"I suppose he can—but I'm not—I don't

know—look," Kahvi took command of herself with an effort, "I can ride this other boat you made. The kids can come with us. We can get back pretty quickly; it's only a few kilos."

Bones thought of several objections, but curiosity about human psychology won out. Ten minutes later the woman, the three children, and a supply of cartridges and food pods were on the larger boat, and the group was moving as fast as the native could drag it back toward the west. Kahvi was explaining everything to the children, and all were looking eagerly or anxiously ahead for the moment when Canton would be visible around the big peninsula.

When it was, the sight was not encouraging. The smoke was still rising. Danna whimpered in terror, and the older children were little better off; their own parents were there too. Kahvi would have liked to be encouraging, but there was nothing very helpful that her conscience would let her say. They could only watch and hope as the meters flowed backward and the scene grew clearer.

It was obvious before they neared the raft that the new building was gone. Smoke was still funneling up from where it had been. The raft appeared intact, however, and it seemed unlikely that any of the prisoners would have been in the lab. Danna looked anxiously at the source of the smoke, but her mother was more interested in the crowd of people. This was far larger than it had been. When she had left, a scant hour before, the forty or fifty adolescents and their captives had been near the jail and along the shore. Now there were at least two hundred, she was sure, though they milled about too much to make counting possible. Were there really this many rebels against common sense and order?

No. She could see now that most of those in sight were barefoot, which was a very good sign. They must be conventional Hillers. What had brought them? And what had happened to the hostages? Kahvi strained to identify faces and forms as the boat drew near, but had not found any she wanted when the slab of foamy tissue slowed and bumped into the suddenly erect form of Bones, a few meters from the beach.

The crowd had seen them coming, and most of its members had turned from the dying fire and spread along the water's edge. Kahvi slowly got off the boat and stood hip-deep, still looking for her husbnad. He definitely wasn't there. Convinced of this, she turned to Bones and signalled briefly, "The children will stay on the boat. Please keep them out of reach of these people until I say it's all right." She repeated the essence of these instructions aloud to the children themselves, and then rather hesitantly began to wade toward the crowd.

Suddenly she saw Viah and Jonathan jostling their way from behind the others, and called to them.

"Your boy is all right. So are the others. Where's Earrin?" The two looked at each other, and Viah finally answered.

"He's hurt, I'm afraid. Some of the delinquents tried to spear him when the rest of the people

showed up. They decided you had sneaked over
the Hill and told about them. I think he'll be all
right, but he has some pretty bad cuts and lost a
lot of blood." Kahvi reached the shore as Viah
finished speaking.

"Where is he?"

"In the jail. The air is still rather high—the
young devils got the cartridge tissue out and the
new spores aren't anywhere near taking over. It
seemed better to give him stronger air when he
had so much blood gone." Kahvi frowned, influenced for a moment by her normal prejudices, but
said nothing. She had to grant the force of the
reasoning.

She started toward the stone building; people
moved aside for her. Most of them were silent;
most had never seen a Nomad. The more conventional and courteous ones could not quite decide
what to say to such a stranger, especially a preg-
nant one. There was some murmuring behind
masks among the more distant members of the
group, but Kahvi couldn't make out the words.

"I take it the Delinquents are under control,"
she said as Viah and her husband reached the lock
with her.

"Yes," the man replied. "When we and Zhamia
and Mort didn't appear back at the city, of course
a group went out to look for us. They saw the
smoke from a distance, and immediately sent
back for still more help—they weren't close
enough to tell whether it was a jail or something
really general. When the big group got here, there
really wasn't much the D's could do, though a

couple of them thought they should keep their promise about killing hostages. I don't know what they've been reading, but they talked about 'matters of principle.' "

"Did they hurt anyone but Earrin?"

"Zhamia was speared, but not as badly damaged as your husband—Mort knocked the fellow out with a rock before he could finish the job. Genda was knocked unconscious, but is awake again and doesn't seem to have changed. The only one of the other side really damaged was the one Mort handled. The others were mostly too smart to fight, and put down their spears."

"After wounding Earrin."

"Of course." Kahvi was silent, then turned to enter the jail.

"Don't tell me which one it was," she said as she went down the steps. "I've already done enough things that made me sick." She ducked under the surface.

Earrin and the other injured ones, except Genda, were on the floor inside, thoroughly bandaged. Her husband was extremely pale, but was conscious and grinned as he saw Kahvi. Disregarding the air, she pulled off her mask, knelt down and kissed him.

"You're sure you're all right," she said when she could finally speak. Nomad honesty dictated the answer.

"No, I'm quite messed up," he admitted. "I seem likely to live, though. It will be quite a while before I can row or pole a raft, I expect." He indicated his left side, where a glass spearhead had severed muscles below the ribs. The arm and leg on the same side were also bandaged. "Yes, it hurts, so restrain yourself—that kiss was fun, but there can be too much of other good things than oxygen."

"At least, the troubles are over for now," she said. "These delinquents who think the rules were made to keep them from enjoying themselves—"

"That's not fair," Earrin pointed out. "They're kids who had trouble believing the same things which you and I haven't believed for a long time either. Seven years ago, Genda would have put you in their class."

"Seven years ago Genda did, the old—scientist. I've been wondering when she'd recognize me, but of course she hasn't seen me indoors yet."

"Don't use *scientist* as a swear word. It distorts your facts. Yes, if Danna's all right, and I assume she is or you wouldn't be in here, the trouble does seem to be over. Of course, we don't have any more orders for glass and such things; we'll have to think of something else the devout Hillers will buy—or maybe you just want to settle down on Milton or at Copper and live on what we can grow and make ourselves."

"There's something to be said for that," the woman admitted, "at least for a few months. Still, roaming around and learning things with Bones is really more fun, and I think it's better for Danna."

"All right. I think I agree, luckily for me. We don't have to settle it completely right now, though. Say, where's Genda? I thought she got hurt in this scuffle, too."

"Not enough—pardon me." Zhamia didn't really sound embarrassed. "She was hit on the head, but seems to be over it. She went outside; she has work to do."

"Oh?" Kahvi and Earrin's voices sounded together.

"She's taking a group to Hemenway to clean out that—laboratory, if you don't mind the word. I guess you Nomads don't very much."

"She doesn't like the idea of a world where you can walk around outdoors without special equipment?"

"Do you?" asked Kahvi, in a tone which Earrin should have recognized.

"It would take some getting used to, I admit," he said slowly. "It would leave a lot of time for other things, though. Just think—"

"I've *been* thinking," Kahvi said firmly. "In the first place, it wouldn't work. I can't believe that anything these young devils planned could really work. They take the easy solution, without caring who gets hurt; and as one of the people who did get hurt, and the mother of another, I'm not impressed by their planning. I know about ecological equilibrium and the population expansion of organisms without natural enemies, but I don't believe this nitrate-reducing spore of theirs can get anywhere. It'll just speed up the nitrate-makers. Anyone knows that sort of interaction. I admit Genda is an irritating woman, but for once I'm willing to help her."

"Tell Bones. Maybe he'll help too," suggested her husband.

"You're joking—but I will. I think you still like the idea, you silly—" Earrin interrupted her with a squeeze from his able arm.

"I do think it would be fun, but credit me with basic common sense," he said gently. "Go ahead and tell Bones—and send him in here afterward, won't you? I'm sure he'd be curious about human physiology as revealed by these spear slashes. He'd like to compare them with what the same weapons did to him and his partner."

"But didn't they kill the other one?" asked Zhamia.

"I doubt it. I'll ask when Bones comes in. Go ahead, Kahv; you know I was only kidding. The risks of a plan like the one these kids were trying out would be far too big, even if it were going to work. I mightn't mind the risks myself, but there's Danna and the next one. We probably wouldn't be alive to worry, ourselves—you're twenty-five already and I'm half a year older. Tell me before you go out—did you learn what caused the fire? I thought it must be Genda acting in line of duty."

There was a laugh from Mort.

"Guess again," he chuckled. "The same thing happened to this lab as to the other one. Credit the kids, Kahvi—one of them did figure it out this time. I'm afraid you wouldn't have sold them any more glass, Earrin. The window panes aren't perfectly flat, you know. They concentrate sun here and there. Plants in the lab, some of them nitrotypes, in a straight oxygen atmosphere—well, it's a surprise the other place lasted as long as it did. One of them was inside this time and saw the blaze start; she was lucky to get out at all. A small start was enough for a big finish. She came screaming out of the lock pool with the story of what was happening, but there was no time for anyone to do a thing before the whole place collapsed. Maybe that'll teach 'em to have all that loose oxygen around. They just weren't trained to be properly afraid of the stuff!"

Kahvi chuckled, too. "Well, maybe by the time they can start over, which won't be very soon if Genda has her way, they'll have figured out some of the rules for themselves so they can believe 'em."

"Maybe," agreed Earrin. "Go on out and tell all that to Bones, too. I don't see how he could possibly work it out for himself, and you know how unhappy it makes him when he doesn't understand something."

"Right. I should tell him that it's all right for the kids to come ashore, too. I'll see you soon; maybe you can come outdoors away from this horrible air before very long."

Earrin smiled quietly as his wife disappeared into the lock pool.

Bones watched for some minutes as the Hillers slowly sorted themselves into small groups and started south. The two families whose children had been threatened were still by the jail with their injured members. The young Delinquents, passive but not entirely resigned, were going back with their elders. It would be interesting to see how these independent minds would develop and perform in the next few years.

But there was work to be done. The Observer

slid into the water and swam quickly toward the
place where the other unit had been left. The job
would take both of them, and both the buds they
would be producing shortly, in the unlikely event
that these proved to be viable copies.

The injured unit was still where it had been left,
moving slowly around in the thicket of seaweed
and occasionally ingesting a mouthful. Bones
sympathized; staying in one place and learning
nothing, as had happened in the Hemenway jail
for so long, was a hideous experience. It was not
surprising that the smaller unit, spotting the
other's approach, showed that it could still swim
rapidly. The pair embraced briefly, and then left
the thicket, swimming at their highest speed toward the south.

South, to the shore where it was closest to
Hemenway. Fast, because they must get there before the human vandals. They must reach the Delinquents' laboratory before it was destroyed and
its contents lost. They knew what to salvage;
Kahvi had told them that. They knew why it had
to be rescued; Earrin, indirectly, had told them
that. They remembered the way.

Even if they were seen coming ashore, it
shouldn't matter; they could travel much faster
than people. No one who saw them would know
what they were doing, until too late.

And once the reducing culture was safe, they
would go into hiding. Their buds would grow, and
separate, and either receive memory or be eaten
for safety's sake; and while this was going on, the
reducing cultures would grow. Presently there

would be enough so that seeding could be expected to take, and spread.

A world with an oxygen atmosphere was interesting even when its existence and qualities could only be inferred. A real one could be watched directly, and the new things to learn would be endless.

The two units swam faster at the common thought.

Gordon R. Dickson

☐ 16015	Dorsai!	1.95	
☐ 34256	Home From The Shore	2.25	
☐ 56010	Naked To The Stars	1.95	
☐ 63160	On The Run	1.95	
☐ 68023	Pro	1.95	
☐ 77417	Soldier, Ask Not	1.95	
☐ 77765	The Space Swimmers	1.95	
☐ 77749	Spacial Deliver	1.95	
☐ 77803	The Spirit Of Dorsai	2.50	

Available wherever paperbacks are sold or use this coupon.

▲ ACE SCIENCE FICTION
P.O. Box 400, Kirkwood, N.Y. 13795

Please send me the titles checked above. I enclose _____.
Include 75¢ for postage and handling if one book is ordered; 50¢ per book for two to five. If six or more are ordered, postage is free. California, Illinois, New York and Tennessee residents please add sales tax.

NAME_____

ADDRESS_____

CITY_____STATE_____ZIP_____

Ursula K. Le Guin

10705	**City of Illusion**	$2.25
47806	**Left Hand of Darkness**	$2.25
66956	**Planet of Exile**	$1.95
73294	**Rocannon's World**	$1.95

Available wherever paperbacks are sold or use this coupon

POUL ANDERSON

MORE TRADE SCIENCE FICTION

Ace Books is proud to publish these latest works by major SF authors in deluxe large format collectors' editions. Many are illustrated by top artists such as Alicia Austin, Esteban Maroto and Fernando.

Robert A. Heinlein	Expanded Universe	21883	$8.95
Frederik Pohl	Science Fiction: Studies in Film (illustrated)	75437	$6.95
Frank Herbert	Direct Descent (illustrated)	14897	$6.95
Harry G. Stine	The Space Enterprise (illustrated)	77742	$6.95
Ursula K. LeGuin and Virginia Kidd	Interfaces	37092	$5.95
Marion Zimmer Bradley	Survey Ship (illustrated)	79110	$6.95
Hal Clement	The Nitrogen Fix	58116	$6.95
Andre Norton	Voorloper	86609	$6.95
Orson Scott Card	Dragons of Light (illustrated)	16660	$7.95

S-15

FAFHRD AND THE
GRAY MOUSER
SAGA

H.
BEAM
PIPER

☐ 24890	**FOUR DAY PLANET/LONE STAR PLANET**	$2.25
☐ 26192	**FUZZY SAPIENS**	$1.95
☐ 48492	**LITTLE FUZZY**	$1.95
☐ 26193	**FUZZY PAPERS**	$2.75
☐ 49053	**LORD KALVAN OF OTHERWHEN**	$2.25
☐ 77779	**SPACE VIKING**	$2.25
☐ 23188	**FEDERATION (5¼'' x 8¼'')**	$5.95